Emerald Knights

Taila Cantrell

Contents

Dedication

For my husband, Tyler, you're support of my author journey has meant the world to me.
And for all the Kings and Queens without a throne.

Quote

If you don't know where you're going, any road will get you there.
-Lewis Carroll

Prologue

From the dream diaries of Eumonia Lyon 1997

I knew I was dreaming. It was the first time I'd ever felt the sensation, but there was no doubt in my mind that I was not awake as I roamed through the woods that surrounded the castle. The light was strange, not from the suns or the moon as it should be. A flickering blue ball caught my attention. Without hesitation, I followed it until I came into a clearing I'd never seen before. I explored the woods that surrounded our castle every day. the newness of this place was exciting. I leaned down, smelling the small white flowers at the edge of the clearing. When I noticed a woman standing in the center, and I hesitated to move forward.

"Come child, be not afraid, for I am your Creator." A strange-looking figure, made of blue light, stood before me. I couldn't make out any of her features; in fact, the only reason I imagined she was a woman was the cadence of the voice that spoke to me. I moved my semitransparent body toward her, "This is your first vision. I implanted it within you, so that when your magick finally awoke, you'd see it."

"My magick is to see?" I tried to keep the disappointment out of my voice. Prophecy magick wasn't flashy. I'd hoped I'd get something more powerful like my father's ability to create illusions or my mother's ability to control water.

"Only a single facet, I have gifted this to you for many reasons. You will be the Queen of Undraland in just a few short years." She offered.

"I'm only ten, ma'am—uh... Creator." I wasn't sure how to address this woman.

"I know, Eumonia, but you will be a great queen to your people. I only need to speak with you now, to give you the tools you will need to fulfill my goals." The Creator waves me toward a seat that had appeared while she'd been speaking. I rushed toward it, tripping over my feet to follow her instructions. I looked toward the woman again. The light that engulfed her body flickered as she bent down in front of me, "Your line has been blessed by my hand. I have shaped a hundred queens before you."

"What about the Red King?" I asked before I could stop myself.

The light flared brighter for a moment causing me to squint, "You are a curious child. That will serve you well on your journey. The Red King was not blessed by me. I am not all powerful, he had control of my world for many, many years before the prophecy came true." I nodded my understanding. The Creator continued, "The world has been at peace for over a hundred years now. There are things coming, and you will be my Queen during these hard times."

"What is coming?" I asked.

"I cannot say, child. The mortal mind can only handle knowing so much. All I ask is that you do not doubt me. I will protect your line with my every move." The Creator said, "There will come a day when you understand what I am asking of you. Remember this, remember that I have given you no pain that I myself do not suffer tenfold."

"You suffer pain? You are the Creator. You're perfect." I said, confused.

A soft laugh left her, "I am your Creator, but I am still imperfect. My powers are limited by my siblings' powers. The only perfect thing in all the universe is love."

Without thinking I stood, throwing my arms around her, "I love you, Creator. I will do anything you ask of me."

A warmth on my back was the last thing I felt before the dream began to fade, "Eumonia, never doubt yourself. You will do great things in your life. Remember I am always with you."

I awoke with a start, rushing from my bed to my parent's chambers. "Mommy, Dada. I know one of my powers." I shouted as I slid down the hallway.

"Monia, darling, the staff isn't even awake yet. Quiet yourself." Mommy said, brushing her dark curls from her face. "Come in. Tell us what you've learned."

I crawled into bed with my father who was rubbing his eyes, "How is my perfect little princess this morning?"

"I spoke to the Creator, Dada." I announced. Both of my parents froze, their eyes wide as they stared at me. I continued, "She told me I'd have other powers, but I'm a seer."

They glanced at each before Dada said, "Are you sure you didn't just have a dream, darling?"

"It was the Creator," I huffed, "She told me I'd be Queen in just a few years." The look of horror on my mother's face caused me to shrink away, "I'm sorry."

"No no. It's okay, Monia. I'm just worried for you... The Creator hasn't appeared to a Lyon Queen since the early days of Undraland." Mommy said.

"You're our special girl. We have to celebrate my daughter's first power!" Dada said, standing from the bed, "Let's go for a ride on the gryphon's."

I jumped up and down on the bed, "Yay."

Mommy still had a strange look in her eyes, but she scooped me up, squeezing me tightly, "I adore you, Eumonia Lyon. Let us go celebrate our girl."

My father's arms were warm as he carried me up the stairs, quietly humming a lullaby that I was far too old for but enjoyed anyway. "Alright sweet, Eu. I think we've done enough celebrating for today. It's time for you to sleep."

"Can we ride gryphons again tomorrow?" I asked, stifling a yawn.

Dada didn't respond as he carefully tucked me into my bed. He smoothed the hair back from my face, pressing a kiss to my forehead, "Princess, get some rest. We will see about the gryphons tomorrow."

Once he left the room I tossed and turned, my mind racing too fast to fall asleep. I wanted to know more about my powers, but my parents had spent the whole day keeping me distracted. I sat up, pushing my blankets away. The library might have more information so I crept to my door, opening it slowly to ensure there were no guards or staff that might catch me. When no one jumped out to tell me to go back to bed, I moved through the hallway, only candlelight from the sconces lighting my way. As I approached the library, hushed voices caught my attention.

"You have to be serious, Demyan. The Creator told her she's going to be queen in a couple of years." My mother hissed. I stopped, though I knew it was wrong to eavesdrop. I wanted to hear what they had to say.

"A couple of years is vague. To a being like the Creator a couple of years could be twenty." My father responded. The clinking of a glass nearly caused me to jump out of my skin. "Stop worrying about an end we cannot foresee, Miriam. We will need to teach Eu that lesson. The future can never be planned for."

"We need to increase her lessons. If I am to die before she reaches adulthood, I will teach her all that I can in whatever time I have left." My mother's words struck me. I had understood what the Creator was telling me, but somehow the reality that my parents would die for me to take the throne didn't compute. My mother continued, even as my eyes filled with tears, "She won't be powerful enough to keep the magick of the realm alive. How can I accept that so easily. How can you?"

"Because I have faith in my daughter. That little girl is wise beyond her years. Hell, she's wise beyond my years. If the Creator has set her down this path, then she will walk it with grace. Whatever happens, I am going to cherish every moment I have left with her..." He trailed off for a moment. The sounds of rustling before muffled words floated to me, "It will be okay, my queen. The Lyon legacy will withstand no matter what."

I backed away from the door, tears and snot running down my face. I ran back to my room, crawling into my bed and hiding under the covers. My parents were my entire world, losing them was unimaginable. I didn't want my powers if it meant I was going to lose them.

PART ONE:

EMERALD KING

Chapter 1

Caterpillar

It was too loud to think, little girl screams, the laugh of the Queen of Hearts. Of Rhosyn. A woman who had been friends with Eumonia before Wonderland was created. I couldn't process that. I could still hear Ilaria's final moments. I couldn't move fast enough, stood in horror as I watched Alice fall into a black hole. Griffin was the only one to move, desperately grabbing at Dina to save her from falling too, but by the time his fingers would have wrapped around her, the hole was gone, and with it the woman I loved. Blood rushed in my ears; I roared, lunging toward the Queen of Hearts, but before I could reach her, she too blinked out of existence. So, I fell to my knees, a broken scream ripping past my lips. Rage clouded my vision. My ears rang, and while activity happened around me, I couldn't think of anything but my wife. The fear in her crystal blue eyes as she fell into a void.

"Roman. Roman. We need to get the children out of here. It's not safe." I heard Rab's voice, knew what he was saying was important, but my only thoughts were the moments just before Alice fell. Her beautiful pale blue wedding dress, our ring on her finger, her perfect blonde hair flowing around her. My wife was gone, and we had no idea where she could be.

The room was silent, shock holding all of our tongues. I could barely think straight. Alice was gone, Ilaria was dead, and Eumonia stood to my left a look on her face I couldn't even begin to describe.

"Rhosyn died. I don't understand..." Her voice trailed off.

"You need to tell us everything about this woman that you know." Alcinda spoke up. I could see rage in her pale golden eyes, but past that I saw the fear. The same fear that made my tongue feel like lead in my mouth. Alice could be dead.

"She was my best friend... my only friend if I'm being honest. Being the Queen of Undraland didn't exactly allow me much time to socialize." She trailed off, "She had portal magick so she was part of my council. When we came to Earth for answers, Rhosyn opened the portal. She wasn't able to make it through. We assumed something terrible had happened."

"Pretty fucking terrible, alright." Cheshire muttered. I looked toward him; He'd taken the time to change out of his suit. His eyes were lined with red, but the determination in them surprised me, "Just to confirm, you're saying that over a hundred and fifty years ago this woman supposedly died trapping you and a bunch of your people here?"

"That's what we were made to believe." Eumonia confirmed, "She was my friend and the only portal magick user of her generation."

"What is portal magick?" Hatter asked.

"It can be a few things, magick isn't one size fits all. Think about how Alice is able to use her electricity manipulation to do things like levitate. It's all about how powerful the magick user is and how they use their abilities." She began to explain. "Portal magick is literal usually, people can open a gateway to another place. It may be as simple as going from one room to the next. But Rhosyn was different, she could open a gate between Undraland and Earth."

"That explains how she was able to disappear so easily." Hatter said, pushing his fingers through his hair, "But that also means Alice could be anywhere."

"Don't forget that Dina and Duchess are also with her." Griffin pointed out, "Dinah doesn't have any way to protect herself against this woman." His rage was as palpable as my own. His wife was gone, and he was powerless. The feeling was bitter on my tongue as well.

"Alice would do anything for Dina, she won't let anything happen to her." Hatter responded.

"We don't know if they're even together. Or where the hell they are. The woman could have dropped them off a cliff in some random corner of Earth for all we know." Cheshire snapped. Hatter ignored his attitude and pulled the smaller man into a hug. I couldn't bring myself to care about how anyone felt. My wife was ripped away from me on our wedding day, and I had no way to help. No answers. No plan. It was my nightmare.

"Caterpillar, we have a bigger problem. The city is going to go into panic when Alice can't make appearances anymore." Alcinda said.

"Fuck the city." I muttered, "We focus on finding Alice."

"The city is going to look to you for answers." She responds.

"I don't fucking care." I snap, standing, "Don't you fucking get it. The Queen of Hearts has won. She ripped Alice away from us."

"Boy, she only wins if you give up." Eumonia said, "I can help with keeping the city calm, but..." She trailed off, looking at Cheshire, "I need you to understand why I've kept this to myself. I have been keeping my secrets for a very, very long time." All of us stare at her as a golden glow engulfed her body, before our eyes Eumonia turned from a hunched over older woman to Alice's identical twin in moments.

"An illusion?" Alcinda asks.

"No. I stopped aging the day that I saved the city." She responds. She looked so much like Alice, I had to force myself not to reach out and touch her. As I examined her, I began to see the differences. Eumonia looked just a bit older, with deeper laugh lines on her cheeks. The shade of her blonde hair is slightly darker, but their eyes are indistinguishable. "For now, I will pose as Alice when it is necessary for the public. At the very least, we can keep up appearances."

"I don't like it." I said before storming out of the room. Looking into Eumonia's eyes after failing to save Alice was going to eat me alive. I had to find my wife. She was my only reason for living anymore.

Chapter 2

Alice

March 16th, 2159

My head pounds in rhythm with my heart, my entire body cracking as I move to sit up. My vision is blurry as I try to take in my surroundings. Everything I look at is strange, I blink my eyes rapidly trying to clear them so I can see better. A yellow sky hangs above me, in strange opposition to the red and blue grass that surrounds me. At first, I believed I was dreaming, until something smacks against my cheek. I curse as a bee-looking creature the size of a small bird falls into my palm. It wiggles for a moment, before taking flight from my hand. A sticky residue covers my palm. I go to wipe it down my pants, only to realize I'm still in my wedding dress. Suddenly, everything clicks, and I remember the moments just before I blacked out. A sob catches in my throat at the visual of Ilaria with a sword shoved through her neck. Poor Caroline. She'd just been reunited with her mother, and now she'd been brutally murdered right before her eyes.

I pushed myself up. Dina and Duchess were standing right next to me, "Dina! Duchess!" I shouted. "Are you out here?"

When no response came I glanced up toward the sky, only to gasp. Two suns hung side by side. It was like nothing I'd ever seen beforc. "Where the fuck am I?" I said aloud. I wracked my brain, until the mural in

Eumonia's home appeared in my mind's eye. Where had she said she was from. Undraland? How was this possible? I was clearly losing my mind. Gone completely mad. I must have hit my head too hard when I fell here. I just couldn't... Being in Undraland meant I was trapped a world away from the men I loved the most. How would I ever get home if I didn't even know how I'd gotten here in the first place? Whatever the Queen of Hearts had done, she'd ensured I had no way out.

I began walking, watching my surroundings carefully as I tried to find any sign of sentient life. It felt like I was walking through this field for hours when I heard a moan. I squatted down, crawling on my knees toward the noise. The grass hid my body.

"Fuck." The voice was familiar, and I stood rushing at Duchess. She screamed when my arms wrapped around her. "Oh, it's you. Thank the Creator. Where the fuck are we?"

"Undraland." I responded, wiping a stray tear from my eye.

"Undraland." She said, dumbly, "Have you lost your mind?"

"It's where magick users are originally from. There's some things I should probably tell you." I realized, rubbing my neck, "But first we need to try to find Dina. She was with us when we fell through whatever the Queen of Hearts did."

Duchess nodded, following me as we continued to walk slowly forward. "Eumonia is my grandmother, well great great great great--"

"I get your point. The woman is a lot older than she looks." Duchess snapped.

"You're not kidding." I muttered. I opened my mouth to speak, but a scream cut me off. I turned toward the noise, and ran. It sounded like Dina. Duchess was hot on my heels as we skidded to a halt in front of a flowing river. At least water looked the same in this world. As I turned to my right I saw Dina across the river, hanging from a tree, caught in a makeshift net. I looked for a way to cross the river, but I didn't see an option, "I'm coming over there, Di. Don't worry."

"That's impossible." She shouted back.

I hiked my dress up, before realizing there was no way to get across the water without soaking it. I sighed, before grabbing the bottom of it, and tearing it until it hung just above my knees. I handed the extra cloth to Duchess, "Hold onto this. It might come in handy later."

The water was freezing, but I pushed myself forward. Thankfully the flow of the river was very calm in this section, so I was able to get across with ease. I rushed toward the tree, but before I could get to Dina, the ground shook, and a huge crater appeared in the way before me. It had a humanoid body and face, but as I backed up, I realized in place of hair its head looked like a mushroom.

It roared at me, taking a step to grab me. I skirted away from it, "Please let my friend go." I shouted.

It paused for a moment, I watched as its mouth moved, but I didn't hear anything. I could tell it was a male from odd beard like thing hanging from it's chin. I moved closer, hoping that I could communicate with it in some way, "My friend can't hang like that much longer. Can you please let her go?"

It didn't seem to understand my intention, because it swung a meaty fist toward my face as soon as I was in range. I managed to hit the ground before it could hurt me. I scampered backward to avoid it's foot slamming into my chest.

"Use your magick, idiot." Duchess shouted from the other side of the river.

She was right of course. I summoned electricity to my fingertips, ignoring the way it rushed to my hand like it never had before. As the large mushroom man got closer to me, I jumped up. It stumbled in surprise, and I used the opportunity to use my magick. I laid a hand on its chest and pumped electricity in as fast as I could. The thing was huge, and I doubted a few zaps were enough to kill it.

It screamed, stumbling away as it's skin rippled. I wasn't prepared for hundreds of tiny mushrooms to fall from the skin where my hand had touched it. I stood in horror as it collapsed to the ground, a strange sobbing noise leaving it's mouth as it picked up the wiggling shrooms from the ground.

"Oh Creator. I'm so sorry." I rushed toward it, reaching to pick up one of the shrooms.

A huge hand fell to my shoulder. My heart raced as I looked into the thing's dark eyes, "Sporekin... does not... know this... language."

"You are Sporekin?" I asked. "I am sorry I hurt you."

He bared his teeth, "I have been the... last Sporekin for... longer than my memory can go... You are... life bringer."

I glanced down at the shroom in my hand, bringing it closer to my face I realized it was a miniature version of the huge creature standing before me, "These are... babies?"

"You have replenished my... society." Huge green tears rolled down Sporekin's face, "I owe you... my life..."

"Uh... That's okay. Could you release my friend?" I said, awkwardly motioning toward Dina.

Sporekin turned, carefully cutting the net down. Dina rushed toward me, dodging around the babies that now wiggled on the ground. "Does this mean you had Sporekin's version of sex?"

I looked at her in horror, "Is that really the first thing you have to say to me?"

"Are you their mother?" She added, a grin curling across her lips.

"I hate you." I muttered, turning back to Sporekin. "We aren't from Undraland. Can you point me in the direction of other people like us?"

It looked at me strangely for a long moment, "Sporekin has not seen others like you in many, many moons... Follow." It motioned for us to follow him. The babies had crawled their way on top of Sporekin's head and now rested atop his red and white head.

We waited for several minutes as Duchess made her way across the river to join us. "Why are we following the huge monster?"

"Don't call Sporekin that. He's just been lonely. We're strangers in his land, have some respect." I corrected her.

Duchess rolled her eyes, but didn't argue. We followed Sporekin through the trees for a long time. It became darker and darker, and I realized that night was falling as we walked. We were all silent as we trekked through the forest, and it gave my mind time to process what had happened. Dina, Duchess, and I were trapped in another world with no way to get home. I was stranded in a new world with no way to get to my husbands... The thought of Caterpillar, Hatter, March, and Cheshire had my feet slowing.

"What's wrong?" Dina asked.

I couldn't even speak as reality set in. I dropped to my knees as the horror filled me. There was no way home, I would never see my husbands again.

Sporekin bent down to me suddenly, laying a huge hand on my back. "Sporekin can feel your pain... We must never... let pain... stop us from... living..." He patted my back hard, "You have... given me a gift today... Come... I will get you to safety."

I took a deep breath, and stood again. We walked for another hour before coming to the largest tree I'd ever seen. It's branches hung low, brushing the top of my head as I passed by. My magick responded, tentatively reaching out to touch the tree. An odd feeling down my spine, but my emotions settled suddenly.

"Enter." Sporekin said, placing his hand on the tree until a door appeared. I stepped forward, glancing inside the tree only to find a huge room. It was nicer than what Eumonia had set up in Wonderland. "You can... rest here..."

"We need clothes." Duchess pointed out. "And a bath."

"The tree will provide..." Sporekin said, cryptically before he stepped inside. I followed him in, completely shocked by the majesty of the space.

A spiral staircase took up most of the entrance, "You'll find… rooms if you follow the staircase."

"How do we know what room is ours?" Duchess asked.

"The tree will tell you." Sporekin responded.

I shrugged and started climbing the stairs. The moment I got the first landing a strange tug in my chest had me taking a hallway to my left. A door with a moon carved into it swung open as I passed. "I guess this is me." I shouted.

"I've found my room too." Duchess shouted back.

Dina stood next to me, looking confused, "What are y'all talking about?"

I furrowed my brows for a moment, "You don't feel it tugging you toward a room?"

She shook her head, "Guess I'm more human than you and Duchess."

I shrugged, "Maybe so. You can bunk with me. I don't think either one of us is used to sleeping alone anyway."

"This may be the first time I've slept through the night in almost two years." She said. Her eyes became distant, "Do you think Elsie is okay? We don't know what the Queen of Hearts did once we ended up here."

"Griffin would never let anything happen to her. Neither would any of the guys. I'm sure everyone is fine." I assured her.

"I hope you're right, Ali." She muttered.

I didn't respond as she went to look for a place to clean up. I had no way of knowing what happened once we fell through to this world, but I had faith in my men. They would find a way to go on, and I would find a way back to them… somehow.

Chapter 3

Cheshire

March 17th, 2159

I was going to kill Caterpillar. It was the only option at this point. If I had to listen to him growl at me one more time I would rip out my perfect hair, "Roman, none of us have anyway of knowing where Rhosyn is. You've been sitting in here for two days. If she pops up on the security cameras I will get an alert."

"I'd rather stay here." He growled back. His face was covered in heavy five o'clock shadow. I was certain he hadn't showered. At least he wasn't still wearing his suit from the wedding. March had managed to get him to change yesterday.

I gritted my teeth and turned around, abandoning my office in favor of some fresh air. I took the stairs to the roof, the sun on my face at least helped relieve some of the stress I'd been feeling. Spring was just about to begin, I had planned to take Alice out into the wildflower fields soon. Instead she was Creator only knows where, and Eumonia had taken up residence in her place so the citizens of Wonderland wouldn't know what happened. I hated it. The urge to disappear had been riding me all day. I'd caught myself fading out earlier, my magick reacting to my emotions. I'd never had a problem like that before, and I had no onc to turn to. I didn't trust Eumonia, Alcinda was a mess, Caterpillar was catatonic, Hatter and

March were functioning, but entirely wrapped up in each other. I had no one to turn to. Alice was the center of our universe, and without her we were completely lost. Thus far the city was still standing, but I didn't have faith that would be true in a few days. The Queen of Hearts had done the one thing that could truly hurt us. She'd taken our wife.

"I'm not surprised to find you up here." Eumonia's voice startled me.

"Why is that?" I asked.

"Other than Roman's prescence in your space? You remind me of the Shadelumes in Undraland. They're similar to Earth's cats in a way, but they are notoriously anti-social unless they bond with someone."

"That doesn't feel like a compliment." I responded, drily.

"You are the most closed off of Alice's men in some ways aren't you? Roman seems that way, but the reality is he loves hard. Hayden and Maxton have always had each other to fall back on." Eumonia continued, ignoring me, "Sinclair, it's okay to feel your feelings."

"Do you know how weird it is that you look just like her? She's gone, and yet you're here pretending to be her." I rambled, "Is your goal to take her place among us?"

"I'm far too old for the likes of you. No, I want my granddaughter home where she belongs just as much as you do." She said. "You won't help her get home by pouting up here."

"I'm not pouting." I snapped.

"Would you rather I call it something manly? Brooding doesn't suit you." She responded. "Get it together, Sinclair. You play just as much of a role in all of this as the others."

"Can't you go lecture Roman?" I sighed. She was right of course, but that didn't mean I liked it.

"In time I'll talk to him as well, but you're far more reasonable than he is." Eumonia said with a smile.

I snorted, "You're right about that."

"I usually am. I'd say Alice is as well. Trust her to get home to you. Right now you need to focus on keeping everyone together."

"Why is that my responsibility?" I growled.

Eumonia looked away from me, stepping onto the edge of the roof. I watched in horror as she shook slightly. "Do you remember when we first met?"

I nodded, "Why don't you get down from there?"

She ignored me, placing each foot in front of the other as she walked, "You heard my story first hand, unlike the other men. Tell me what you thought about what you learned." Her body tilted slightly, but she just laughed and continued on.

I wracked my brain trying to remember that day, "I thought... Alice was a queen without a throne."

Eumonia turned her head to look at me, "What does that make you as her husband?" Her foot slipped, and I didn't think as I rushed to grab her before she slipped over the edge. I sat her back on the roof, my heart pumping fast. "Answer the question, Sinclair."

"A king." I panted, "It makes me her king."

"You are all her kings. You need to start acting like it." Eumonia said, gripping my shoulder.

"Why did you need to give me a heart attack to say that?" I asked.

"Because you wouldn't have listened otherwise." She said, before leaving me alone again.

Strangely enough, I knew she was right. I didn't entirely trust Eumonia, I certainly respected her. The illusion she'd used to appear as an old woman still haunted me. The truth was I couldn't deal with how much she reminded me of Alice. The woman I loved... the woman I had failed. I didn't know if I would ever see her again, to apologize for not doing more. I shook my head. Alice would want us to keep it together, to care for each other and protect Wonderland until she found her way back. She would find her way back, I had no doubt about that anymore.

Today I would act like the king that Alice deserved.

Being a king was harder than I'd expected. My jaw throbbed from the punch Caterpillar had landed when I'd tried to drag him from my office.

"That was stupid." Hatter said, handing me a bag of ice, "What were you thinking?"

"He needs to get out of that room. Alice needs us to take care of Wonderland in her stead. Sitting in there isn't going to fix anything." I ranted.

Hatter and March exchanged a look, before Hatter replied, "That is a... very mature stance. Cheshire, our wife is gone. Possibly... dead."

March cringed, "She c-c-can't be."

I gritted my teeth, "I know she isn't. She's somewhere out there, trying to make her way home. We will find a way to get to her, but in the meantime we need to get our heads on straight."

"It's only been two days." Hatter argued.

"Unfortunately he's right." Caterpillar's voice boomed through my pounding skull, "Sorry, Ches. I shouldn't have hit you."

"It's fine." I muttered.

"It isn't. I am supposed to be the leader around here. Thank you for trying to help." He responded.

"No one expects you to be perfect all the time. We can take some of the burden as well." Hatter chimed in, "We lost our wife, you aren't alone."

We all stood in silence before finally, March stood pulling us all into a hug. It was awkward at first since Alice wasn't here, but it didn't take long for each of us to cry. Alice was our world, not a single one of us was going to be okay when we had no idea what was happening to her. But I could hold us accountable. I would be the King our Queen deserved.

Chapter 4

Alice

March 22nd, 2159

We stayed in the tree for several days, eating and trying to come up with a plan to find a way home. Duchess was no help, certain that we would never get back home. She had decided that she'd stay with Sporekin, but as I stood from the dining table in frustration I said, "I'm leaving today. Staying here will not get me back to Wonderland."

"When will you accept that there's no way back?" Duchess snapped at me.

"Never. I will find a way home with or without you. Dina and I can travel around until we find someone who might be able to help us." I argued.

Duchess and I stared at each other for a long time, before she stormed out of the room. "We shouldn't leave her here." Dina said once she was gone.

"I know, but I can't force her to go with us." I sighed, returning to my seat. "How are you doing?"

Dina looked down at her hands, "I miss Elsie and Griffin. Being away from them is worse than being held by the Red Queen."

I cringed, "I'm sorry, Di. I promise I will find a way home."

She shook her head, "It's not your fault we're here, Ali." It was, but I wasn't going to argue with her. If I had found a way to kill the Queen of

Hearts this wouldn't have happened. I should have tried harder to figure out the truth. Now all three of us were trapped here away from our loved ones. There was no one else to blame but me. "It's not worth blaming yourself. We will find a way out of this situation." Dina continued.

Before I could respond, Sporekin appeared, "Come." He'd clearly picked up a decent amount of our language, but the strange creature wasn't always easy to communicate with. I guess if you've always been alone, communicating wasn't something you had to learn how to do. We both stood to follow him. I noticed one of the baby Sporekins sitting on his shoulder, staring at me with bright orange eyes. It waved a tiny hand at me as we followed, something about it's adorable innocence warmed my aching heart.

"How are your babies doing?" I asked.

"The tiny sporekin's thrive within the tree." Was his only response. I could tell he didn't entirely trust us, so I decided not to push any further. He brought us to the exit from the tree, "You plan to leave in search of... others like you." I nodded, though it was more a statement than a question, "You will need... armor." Sporekin went to a door I hadn't noticed when we entered and swung it open. Dina gasped as we peaked inside, the room was full of decorative armor of all sizes, weapons I couldn't even begin to name, even two crowns sat on pedestals. Without thinking I approached them, my magick buzzing as I drew closer. One crown was golden, embedded with gems in deep blues and greens. I ran a finger over one of them, but moved to the other crown, my magick thrashing wildly as I inspected it. It was silver, vines and leave made up the base, only a milky white gem was laid in the center. It reminded me of the tiara I'd worn at my wedding. I had no idea what had happened to it once I'd fallen through the portal. As I went to pick up the crown that called to me the lights in the room flickered, a strange groaning noise filled the room. When I placed it on my head the room went black, only the electricity racing down my arms provided light. My body was frozen as my magick reacted to the magick within the crown.

A melodic voice filled my ears, *"Welcome home, daughter."*

The lights returned to normal, my ears ringing as my magick resettled into my chest, I turned to find Sporekin kneeling, "Sporekin did not know you were a Lyon."

My eyes widened, "Sporekin, please stand up. I'm just Alice."

"Ali, you... didn't you hear the voice that spoke?" Dina asked, an ashen look on her face.

I nodded, "It's... a lot. Why don't we get some armor." I couldn't even begin to process what had just happened. I certainly didn't want to tell Dina that my magick felt different... more potent than it ever had before. The situation was bad enough.

"I was a youngling when the last Lyon Queen disappeared." Sporekin spoke as Dina and I shuffled through the many materials that could be used as armor. A pair of brown pants made of a material similar to leather caught my eye. "Undraland isn't the same place it was then."

"What's changed?" I asked, finding a simple white shirt that looked like it would fit me.

"There is sickness... creatures aren't the same as they were before." He responded.

"You seem okay." Dina said.

"Sporekin is immune to the sickness, it took the rest of my kind." Sporekin's voice cracked as he spoke, clearly overcome by emotion. "The little spores are a great blessing... A sign that the Creator has blessed your rule."

"I'm not interested in ruling anyone." I sighed, "Sporekin, I have to find my way home. My family isn't in Undraland."

Sporekin nodded, staring at me for a long moment, "May the Creator guide you. I will escort you to a safe location, but I must return here to raise my spores."

"We understand." I said, grabbing a hand full of clothes that looked like something Duchess might like, "Give us an hour and we can leave."

Somehow Dina and I managed to convince Duchess to join us. With new clothing and weapons in hand we followed Sporekin out of the tree that had given us protection for several days. My eyes had to adjust to the sheer amount of sunlight that the two suns provided. I hadn't really noticed how bright they were that first day, but now it made my eyes hurt. I glanced at Duchess who looked completely relaxed in the deep green matching leather garments we'd found to fit her. Dina had elected a strange looking skirt and top that shined in the sun, making me wonder if there was metal woven into the fabric. I hoped we wouldn't have to test how well it could protect her.

I had removed the crown I'd put on my head, but I couldn't bring myself to leave it behind, it sat in the top of the bag that Sporekin had shoved into my arms before we'd left. Duchess and Dina each carried a replica of the bag. I hadn't taken the time to look through it, but I'd noticed several bags of strange looking berries and a substance I hadn't been able to identify. We walked through the woods for hours, I could hear the sounds of creatures moving about, but none approached us. When we finally made it out of the woods, we weren't at the river and field that we'd met Sporekin at. A dirt road stretched ahead of us, or at least it looked like a dirt road, if dirt was usually a deep purple color.

"Following this road will lead you to the Queen's castle." Sporekin informed us, "It is a dangerous journey, but hopefully what you seek can be found there."

"The Queen's Castle?" Duchess echoed. "That feels like the worst possible place to go."

"Thank you for your help, Sporekin. If we don't meet again, I hope the baby spores grow big and strong." I said, ignoring Duchess.

"We will meet again, Queen Alice." I cringed at his words. We all waved at him as he lumbered back into the woods.

Once he had disappeared, and the three of us stood alone staring down the dirt trail ahead I spoke, "Our only choice is to travel until we meet someone who can help us find a way home."

"There is no way home." Duchess grumbled, but I elbowed her in the ribs, nodding to Dina who looked stricken at her words. Duchess looked ashamed, "Sorry, Dina. I'm just... a real bitch I guess."

"That's nothing new." Dina responded, "At least the Queen's castle will probably have actual people in it."

I considered her words, I wasn't as certain as she was that we would find people like us, but I didn't want to tell them my fears. That we were the only humans in all of Undraland. What had happened to the people that Eumonia left behind? Surely some had survived... but as my mind wandered back to all of what I knew about Undraland I cringed. Eumonia had said there was a strange sickness in the land. Maybe it had wiped most people like us out.

We walked for hours, until the suns began to sit lower in the sky. As darkness descended the night came alive, noises that had seemed innocent in the daytime had all three of us jumping. Undraland was nothing like Wonderland, even when the Red Party had been in charge, I'd never been afraid to walk the streets.

"Did we have a plan for where we are going to sleep?" Duchess asked, "It's not as if we're going to find a hotel out here."

"Sporekin said our bags should have something in them for shelter overnight." Dina responded. A bead of sweat dripped from her forehead causing me to furrow my eyebrows. The temperature had dropped significantly in the last few hours. It wasn't cold by any means, but it also wasn't hot. It was probably just all the walking she'd been doing.

"Let's set up camp at the edge of the woods here. The trees will give us some cover overnight, but we'll still be close to the road." I suggested.

No one argued with my suggestion, so we set up camp in silence. When we all had our bed rolls laid out around a blazing fire Dina pulled out some food from her bag, "We should eat and then go to sleep. Maybe we can get up at first light and make more progress tomorrow." When Duchess and I both nodded our agreement, Dina began to carefully unwrap the strange pieces of meat and vegetables. None of them were familiar to us, but one did seem to have a similar consistency to potatoes after it cooked. Duchess wouldn't touch the slightly glowing spears that reminded me of aspargus, which caused all of us to laugh. We may be stuck in a strange world with no way home, but Duchess' tastes wouldn't change.

A yawn escaped me as I leaned back, my belly full, "That was pretty tasty, Di. Thank you."

"I'm going to take first watch. You should both get some sleep." Duchess announced, cutting off any further conversation.

"You don't need to do that, I can stay up." I argued.

"You're already yawning and Dina looks exhausted. Sleep, I'll wake you up in a few hours." She said.

I glanced to Dina, noticing the drawn look on her face I decided to curl up next to her. The bedrolls were more cushioned than I expected, so it was easy to drift into a light sleep.

A boot pressing into my chest brought me out of my sleep. I opened my eyes, taking note of Duchess' position first. Her mouth was full of fabric, but her eyes burned in anger as she stared at the man that kept me immobile. I called my magick, wrapping electricity around my hand, I grabbed the leg of the man who stood on me. He crumpled to the ground in seconds, shouting in a language I didn't recognize. In the dark it was hard to see, but another figure stood over Dina, so I moved, knocking a second man away from her. Magick pounding through my body like it never had before. I couldn't let myself consider what it meant for my magick to be this much stronger now.

A third man appeared behind Duchess, holding a blade to her neck. He spoke again, but I didn't understand what he wanted. "Let her go." I growled.

The two men I'd managed to injure got to their feet. A conversation passed between them before one of them lifted his grip on Duchess.

"You speak the Queen's language. Who are you?" The man's voice was low, almost hard to hear.

"My name is Alice--" I started to say.

"I told you she's the one." A different voice interjected.

Everyone was silent for a moment before I said, "Listen, we're from Earth. We don't want any problems, we'd just like to get back home."

"We are obligated to assist the Queen." The same man said, before I could protest he continued, "You chose a very unsafe spot to rest. We will guard you while you sleep as is our duty. At first light we will begin guiding you to the Queen's Castle."

I sighed, too tired to argue with him. I glanced between Duchess and Dina, both of them looked shaken and exhausted. "If harm comes to either of my friends, I'll make those little zaps feel like kisses from your mothers."

All three men nodded before they moved into positions across the camp. I helped Dina over to her bedroll noticing the way she shook as she laid down. Duchess was already laying down when I turned to speak to her, so I climbed back into my bedroll. It was harder to fall asleep this time, surrounded by strange men in a strange land, but eventually exhaustion overtook my mind and I rested.

Chapter 5

Hatter

March 24th, 2159

The wind in my face was the only relief from the anxiety that filled every waking moment. It had been almost ten days since Alice disappeared, and while Cheshire's kick to the ass had helped it didn't give us any ideas on what to do. All of our people in the boonies were scouring around Wonderland to see if there was any trace of Alice or the Queen of Hearts. So far they had turned up nothing. My feet pounded the ground harder as I pushed myself beyond my normal, my lungs beginning to squeeze from lack of oxygen. At least there was silence in the woods. As I approached the cliff, for a single moment I considered jumping.

I shook my head, ridding myself of the dark thoughts. March still needed me, Alice was still alive, there was no reason to give up yet. I stripped my shirt off, running my fingers over the tattoo I'd gotten when I'd turned eighteen. I got it more as a reminder for March than for myself. *Non desistas non exieris.* Never give up, never surrender. March never had in all truth, even now, as I watched the light start to fade from his eyes there was a part of him that couldn't let the darkness win. I had always admired that about him.

I paced around, realizing this was the exact spot I'd brought Alice to just a few weeks ago. That afternoon had been fun, easy even. I wanted that back in ways that I couldn't explain. I just had to hold out hope, not just for me, but for March too. Alice would make it back to us, we would find our wife... No matter what it cost.

Alice

The Emerald Knights were quiet as we walked. They refused to give us any information about themselves, not even their real names. I'd taken to calling them a, b, and c when I had to refer from them. They were a perfect matched set in their dark green and black armor. The helmet they wore had to be hot under the two suns, but they never took them off. Even when we sat down to eat they would disappear into a different clearing alone. Duchess had started to go after them to see what they were hiding, but I had stopped her. We didn't understand the culture here; I didn't want to cause them a problem if I didn't have to. They had been kind to us for the most part. Apparently, we were still several days away from the Queen's Castle. I wasn't certain that what we needed would be found there. Hell, I wasn't even sure what we needed to get home, but at least we had somewhere to look.

"We will rest here for tonight. The Noxroot's don't usually inhabit this section of the woods." The tallest knight said as we made our way off the path.

"The what?" Dina asked, glancing nervously toward me.

"They are one of Undraland's creatures. Since the disappearance of Queen Eumonia they have become... angry about trespassers in their forest." A different knight responded. This was b, he was my favorite of them, providing tidbits of information anytime we asked.

"Would they harm us?" I asked, glancing around the area we were in. The forest here was made up of trees with trunks the size of a small car. Leaves and branches hung low, a few holding sparkling green fruit. I watched as the tallest knight picked several pieces, dropping them into a small leather pouch on his belt.

"Unfortunately, anything in Undraland may harm you right now. It's extremely unsafe." Knight A said, "But you don't need to worry, it is our job to ensure the safety of the Queen." I'd given up trying to argue with them that I was not the next Queen of Undraland. Once I returned home maybe they would understand. I felt a stab of guilt at the idea of abandoning them to this world, it was clear there were very few magick users like me left here.

"That doesn't make me feel any better." Duchess muttered.

Knight C stopped his quiet inspection of some of the green fruit, "You accompany a Queen. Try acting like it."

My eyebrows raised at his harsh words. Duchess stopped walking, staring at him for a moment, "You do realize that we don't even know your names right? If you're so loyal to your Queen why hide who you really are."

Silence filled the small area. She was right, traveling with three strange men who kept their faces covered and their names hidden didn't sit well with me. I just accepted that we needed some kind of help regardless of who they were. My magick didn't buzz beneath my skin as if we were in danger.

"You question my loyalty to the crown?" The Knight growled back at her, "You're a selfish, spoiled brat."

"Okay, okay. Name calling isn't appropriate. We're all feeling tired, why don't we set up camp." Knight A said. Duchess' face was red, but she didn't say another word as we all set up our bedrolls to rest for the night.

Once we were all laid down with our stomachs full the exhaustion hit me. Within moments I was drifting off into a dreamless sleep.

A groaning noise and a loud crash had my eyes popping open suddenly. The fire one of the knights had built was out, causing a chill of fear to run down my spine as I squinted into the darkness. I sat up, whispering into the darkness, "Duchess, Dina?"

There was no response, so I stood, calling my magick to my hand in hopes of lighting the darkness. I regretted it the moment my eyes landed on one of the knights, head lolled to the side. I couldn't see any blood, but that didn't mean he wasn't harmed. I continued looking around, barely moving a muscle. Another groaning noise had me spinning around, barely ducking under a giant branch as it swung at my face. I stumbled away, barely stopping the scream that was working its way up my throat as I laid eyes on the towering tree. When I met its eyes, my vision swam. The red orbs stood out in the night. I found my footing again, turning to run as the creature cocked back its branch like arm for another swing. I didn't make a noise as I frantically searched for anyone that was conscious. Arms wrapped around my waist, yanking me out of the path of a third swing.

"Careful my queen. Noxroot's see very well in the darkness." One of the knight's voice filled my ears. "Stay here, I have already moved your friends to a safe place."

Before he could run off I grabbed his arm, "You can't fight that thing alone."

"It is my duty, my queen." He responded.

"I am not your queen." I snapped, "I am just another person, use me... my powers to run it off."

He was silent for a long moment, "It won't fear your electricity. Do you have anything else?"

"I can create illusions." I bit my tongue before I told him about my other power. I didn't exactly trust him yet.

"That could be helpful... Could you mimic sunlight?" He asked, a note of excitement in his voice. "The Noxroot sleep during the day, it might lull the creature to sleep."

I thought for a moment. It wasn't something I'd ever tried, but surely I could find a way. "Give me time to figure it out."

The Knight moved away, leaving me alone with my thoughts. I hadn't trained my illusion magick as much as I should have. I never regretted it more than I did now. I forced myself to take a deep breath, clearing my mind. First, I pictured the sun as it shined down on my head in my wildflower field in Wonderland. I imagined the warmth growing in my hands. Then I pictured the two suns that beat down on us as we've traveled through Undraland. Their brightness and heat was so different from Earth, yet I'd come to appreciate them the same way I did Earth's sun. When I opened my eyes, my hands held a ball of glowing light so bright my eyes started to water.

I let out a sigh of relief, but my momentary success was drowned out by a pained shout. I ducked around the tree, holding my hands up in hopes that any of the creatures would be too afraid to attack. As soon as I stepped out into our camp a shriek of fear cause my ears to ring. The ground shook as two of the creatures ran from me, one nearly falling over one of the Knight's to get away. I didn't let go of my illusion as I ran to check on the Knights. Two of them were barely standing, but the one who had saved me stepped forward.

"Good job, my queen. The Noxroots won't come back tonight. I'll bring your friends back to camp, and then get the boys patched up." He said, my light reflecting off his metal armor, "You can let the illusion go now."

"At this point, can you please tell me your names. I'm tired of not knowing how to refer to you." I said, ignoring the way my magick fought against being let go. It was stronger, and I still hadn't learned to manage it's resistance. The call to constantly use magick swirled in my gut in a way it never had before. It was damn near addicting anytime I called it forth.

The Knight sighed, "My name is Edik." He pointed toward the smallest of the three knights, "That is Kori. And the behemoth is Ledger. It is against our code to remove our helmets before a royal, so you'll have to excuse our customs. I know they must seem strange to you."

I nodded, "Thank you, Edik. I can respect the vows you've taken as knights."

He inclined his head, before turning to help Kori and Ledger to their feet. Once they were moving on their own, they brought Dina and Duchess from wherever they had been hiding, "Get some rest, ladies. We will move at first light. We're only two more days from the Queen's castle now."

Sleep didn't come easily to me this time, but as I drifted off, I thought of my own men, wondering how Wonderland fared with me gone. I hoped that the Queen of Hearts wasn't wreaking havoc on the guys while I was away.

Chapter 6

March

March 26, 2159

I was miserable. Truly, irrevocably miserable. Hatter was barely keeping it together. Caterpillar and Cheshire were on the warpath, desperate to find Alice. I was useless. I missed my wife, and yet there was nothing that I could do to help find her. I wasn't a genius hacker or badass leader of the Resistance. I was just the March Hare, just Maxton Danara. I had no useful skills other than some mild medical training. I was impulsive, too soft, and completely lost without Hatter and Alice guiding me.

Today, my misery was only made worse by the rain that had suddenly started to fall on my walk back home. I'd picked up a few groceries so that I could at least make sure everyone ate. Now I was soaking wet. The rain had even soaked through my boots and into my socks. It couldn't get any worse. The bags I carried were barely holding together under the onslaught of rain.

I knew the moment the thought popped into my head I would regret it. As I turned the corner I slammed into someone, causing me to drop the paper bags I was carrying.

"I'm s-so s-s-sorry." I had to force myself not to wail out my misery as I knelt to try to gather my groceries.

"Maxton?" My mother's grating voice made me freeze. Any thoughts blanked out from my mind as I blinked up to see her standing above me, bright pink umbrella in hand. Her tracksuit today was teal with yellow accents, the mixture of colors making her look like a strange bird. She snorted, "I guess being married to the leader of Wonderland doesn't come with any perks. I can't believe she would have you out here in this rain running her errands." I bit my tongue to stop myself from reminding her of the time that Martin had left me out in a thunderstorm for three days because I'd snuck a peanut butter sandwich because I hadn't been allowed to eat. I stood without saying a word, barely able to hold onto the groceries since the bag had disintegrated on the pavement. I tried to skirt around her, but she blocked my path, "I am your mother, Maxton. I don't know what brainwashing Hayden and Alice have done on you, but I've only ever looked out for your best interests."

"You let your boyfriend sell me to the highest bidder like I was cattle." I growled, "In what world do you think that was for the b-best?"

She paled, but still managed to retort, "I didn't know what he was doing to you, Maxie. I was high. Surely you can find a way to forgive me?"

"I would almost believe that, if you weren't still such a fucking cunt." I snapped, rage eating me alive, "You've done nothing but manipulate and abuse me. I told you I don't want anything to do with you."

Her mouth opened and closed, her cheeks turning bright red as she sputtered to think of a response. Before she could a new voice drew our attention, "Claudia?"

A strangely familiar man crossed the street, his eyes set on my mother, "Claudia, I've been looking for you for years!"

My mother spun around, "You..." She glanced to me, but squared her shoulders, "I told you I never wanted to see you again."

The anger on the man's face surprised me, "Where is my son? You've kept him from me his entire life, at least tell me his name."

My brows furrowed, but before I could put together what he had said my mother turned on me, "You know what, Maxton... Henry, this is your son." Before me or the other man could respond, my mother turned on her heel and stormed away.

"I-I-I-I..." I choked, staring into the face of the man who now looked at me with a strange amount of warmth. I understood what she had implied, but my brain was short circuiting. This man was my father? He extended his hand, but I couldn't move. I was completely frozen as the world spun around me.

"Woah there. I'm sorry. I know--" Whatever else he was going to say was lost as my world turned and went black.

I came awake with a gasp, my eyes darting in every direction of the unfamiliar bedroom I was in. Rain pelted the windows, making me glance down at my clothes. I was no longer in the jeans and sweater I'd that had been soaked through. Instead, I wore a comfortable pair of black joggers and a soft green t shirt. Panic crawled up my throat, nearly blinding me. My breath came in sharp pants that I couldn't control. I stood, stumbling toward the outline of the door. I threw it open, gripping the doorjamb as I glanced down the short hallway.

The smell of citrus cleaner met my nose, but there were no other sounds or smells to clue me in to where I was. My heart squeezed uncomfortably causing me to gasp. The door directly across from me opened, and the man from the street appeared. The glasses he wore were slightly askew as he met my eyes. "Oh, I'm glad you're awake. You took a pretty hard fall. Are you okay?"

I opened my mouth to respond, but no words would come out. The man stepped forward, laying a hand on my shoulder. Instantly the panic I'd been feeling melted away, "You're safe here. I promise that I mean you no harm. I think we should sit down and talk." His words caused some calm to wash over me.

"O-okay." I responded, allowing him to lead me into a sparsely decorated living room. There were only two chairs and a small table in the large space. He sat down, motioning for me to do the same.

Once I took a seat, he began to weave a story, "My name is Henry Tinniel. Many years ago, I dated Claudia Danara. Back then I was young and naive. I didn't see her strange behaviors for what they were. Claudia was sick in the mind. She had good days, and on those days, it was easy to forget just how bad her bad days really were. At least until she got pregnant." I stopped breathing as the story unfolded. A piece of my past that had been hidden from me, "I hardly ever left her side during her pregnancy. Regardless of how her father felt about me, I was determined to take care of her and our child. However, Claudia became increasingly erratic as her pregnancy progressed. Just a couple of weeks before her due date she disappeared from our apartment. I didn't see her again for five years. When I finally did she had her boyfriend at the time attack me. I'm sorry, Maxton. I did look for you, but she kept you locked away, I didn't even know your name until she told me today." He sighed, "I've managed to lose both of my sons."

Suddenly, his familiarity clicked into place, "You-you're Lewis' father as well!" I jumped up, pacing the floor, "We hunted for you, but we couldn't find you anywhere. Lewis is s-safe with my wife's mother."

A grin broke across Henry's face, and before I could prepare myself, he grabbed me into a crushing hug, "This may be the best day of my life." I was stiff for only a moment, before I melted into his arms like a child. This was my father. A father who wanted me, who would have protected me. In a few short sentences he had fused back together parts of me that had been broken my entire life. "I want to see Lewis as soon as possible, it's been over a year since he last saw me. But first... please tell me all about your life."

"What did you do with my phone?" I asked, realizing I needed to let Hatter know where I was.

"Here is everything I took out of your pockets. I did my best to save some of your groceries as well. They're in the fridge when you're ready to leave." Henry said, handing me everything that had been in my pockets. I slipped my wallet and keys into my sweats. When I tried to turn my phone on, it flashed, showing cracks across the entire screen.

I sighed. Caterpillar wouldn't be happy, but at least we had plenty of backups. I considered for a moment what I should do. I didn't want to cut this conversation short, but I knew that Hatter would worry if I didn't show up for our usual gym night. Things were tense at home, but I knew I deserved a chance to speak with my father alone. Hatter would understand. Ultimately, I decided to prioritize myself this time. I needed to talk to my father. Hatter would understand. "Do you have m-magick?" I blurted out, causing my father's eyes to widen.

"Why don't we take a sit again?" Henry responded, "I take it you have discovered your own magick? How did it manifest?"

I gulped. I didn't want to tell him. What if he hated me for what I could? "I can emotionally manipulate people to do what I want? My wife j-jokes that my puppy dog eyes are literally magickal."

Henry was silent for a moment, studying me, "The magick users in Wonderland nicknamed me the Poet a very long time ago. My abilities manifest in a way that allows me to inspire people no matter how horrible they feel. When someone was sick or unable to keep up with the workload, they called for me. I gave a speech. They hopped up and did their job. It wasn't how I would like to use my abilities, but it kept a lot of people alive during those dark times." I was impressed; it sounded like the core of our abilities were similar. "I don't think you should consider it a form of manipulation. So long as you're only using it to improve the lives of the people around you, it isn't an evil power. Nothing like what the Red Queen could do." He shivered, his face paling as he mentioned her name.

Tears filled my eyes, but I refused to let them fall. For the first time in my life I was understood. "I'll t-try to keep that in mind."

"This is rude to ask… Have you always had the stutter?" I flinched at the question. I couldn't stop myself. I'd been ridiculed for my speech impediment my entire life. I didn't know if I could take it if he did the same thing. "I only ask because my mother also had a stutter. It must be hereditary." He rushed to say, "I loved the sound of her voice. I don't want you to think for a moment that it makes me think any less of you."

I couldn't stop the tears from falling down my face now. "Th-thank you."

"I don't know what kind of life you've had, Maxton. I know it can't have been easy with Claudia as your mother. I hope you'll give me the chance to show you that I care for you." He said, reaching across the distance and patting my shoulder, "Now you've mentioned your wife. Please tell me all about her. I'd love to meet her soon."

"You've actually already met her." I couldn't tell him the truth about our situation just yet. Any of it. "She was the woman you gave Lewis to. Alice Young."

His lips formed an 'o', "I've heard her name, but I didn't realize… She makes you happy?"

"More than I've been in my entire life." I admitted.

"Then I can't wait to meet her and thank her for taking good care of both of my sons." He grinned.

Slowly, I relaxed in my chair. We chatted for hours until the rain had stopped, and darkness was descending on the city. With every new detail I learned about him I understood myself more. I had always been loved, even though he had never met me, he had been out there searching. "I n-need to get going."

"I understand. Please take my number, let me know when we can meet again. I also want to see Lewis as soon as is reasonable." He said, escorting me to the door.

"I will." We embraced for a long moment before I began the long trek home, groceries weighing down my arms once again. I walked quickly, realizing I'd been gone far, far longer than I should have been without checking in with someone.

As I turned the corner to our apartment I slammed into a hard body, "March! Where the ever loving fuck have you been?" Hatter's voice pitched higher in his panic. "We've been calling and looking for you for hours. You can't just disappear right now." He hissed, dragging me by my bicep into the building. "Hold on I've got to call Caterpillar, he's out on the bike looking for you." Caterpillar answered on the first ring, "He's here... Yes... Seems like it... Yup, see you in a bit."

"I'm s-sorry." I said, seeing the anger set on Hatter's face as he turned back to me.

"Sit those down." He commanded, pacing the floor. I carefully put away each item, giving him time to cool off. "Where have you been?"

"I r-ran into Claudia." Hatter's jaw tenses and he opened his mouth to say something. I held my hand up, "It's fine. I'm fine. I met my real father." He stopped pacing at that, his anger melting away, "He's a magick user. He's been looking for me years. There's so much more, b-but... yeah. He's also Lewis' father."

At that Hatter's dark green eyes widened, "Was he kind to you?"

"Yes. I want you to meet him soon, but we need to discuss what he can know about our... s-situation before that." I said.

"I'm happy for you, March. I really am, but why didn't you let me know where you were. I've been panicking for hours."

"I'm s-sorry. My phone broke. I didn't think I'd be gone so long, I swear." I responded.

Hatter pulled me into arms, burying his nose into my hair. "I love you so much, Maxton, but sometimes I think you're going to be the death of me."

"I love you too, Hayden. I really am sorry." He looked at me for a long minute.

"Come with me. We have some time before Caterpillar gets back." I rushed to do as he asked, knowing the look of lust in his eyes. "Strip, get on the bed on your hands and knees. We both need this, it's been too long, but you will not cum tonight. That's your punishment for not even trying to let someone know where you were." I nodded vigorously, doing as he said. My cock ached, but I loved Hatter's dominance. I would do anything he wanted.

He ran his hands over my ass, before he smacked his hand down. I grunted, ignoring the way the pain only made me harden further, "Hard and fast, baby. That's what I need."

"Do it." I panted. With those words, he pushed into my ass. The stretch burned since he hadn't prepped me to take him, but I powered through knowing even that was part of my punishment. I loved it. His hips snapped into mine rubbing against my prostate until tears ran down my face from holding off my orgasm.

"I am going to cum in your tight little ass, Max." Hatter groaned.

"Please, Hayden, please." I cried, moments from falling apart regardless of his commands. Finally, I felt his climax fill me. His moans went straight to my weeping dick, but I was happier that I'd followed his commands. He pulled out and rushed to the bathroom. When he came back, he used a warm, wet cloth to clean me up before helping me redress in my own clothes. "I love you." I said, pulling him into a kiss.

"You're a good boy, March." He muttered, refusing to release me, "I hope meeting your father helps you."

"It really has." I admitted. I felt more settled than I had in my entire life. I wasn't perfect, but for the first time I truly felt like I was the right path to truly healing from everything I had been through. Meeting my father was the closure I had aways needed.

Chapter 7

Alice

March 28th, 2159

I was tired of walking. When I got back to Wonderland, I was going to make the guys carry me around like the Queen everyone claimed I was. My calves screamed from exertion, sweat dripped down my spine. Dina and Duchess were no better off. We all looked like we'd been awake and walking through the woods for days. That wasn't far from the truth, but at least we were about to cross the bridge that would take us to the Queen's Castle.

"The bridge has broken down with the years of disuse. A knight will escort each of you across just in case." Edik said, "Ledger you take Duchess. Kori, you're with Dina. I will escort the... Alice." At least he was trying to respect that I was not the queen he saw me as.

Ledger was the hulking knight that grunted more than he spoke. Without another word, he reached down, lifting Duchess onto his shoulders and taking the first steps across the bridge. It swayed with their weight, the wood creaking loudly as they slowly made their way across. Once they were safely on the other side, Kori, my favorite of the three knights took Dina's hand. They moved slowly, their steps careful, but they made it across without any problems.

"Are you ready?" Edik asked, giving me his hand.

"If anything happens to me, it is your duty to care for my friends. Try to get them home." I said, trying to keep my voice light. I'd had the thought several times over the last few days, but I had never been alone with the knight to make this demand.

"I cannot--" He started.

"You will swear it to me as your Queen." I cringed at using his oaths against him, but I needed to be sure that if I died or was lost that the knights would still care for Duchess and Dina.

"I swear to you that I will let no harm befall your friends, my Queen." He gritted out, before offering me his arm.

I forced myself to look straight ahead, ignoring the sheer drops on either side of the bridge. I could hear water rushing below, but I couldn't look. My grip on Edik's cool armor was enough to nearly dent the metal. A scream worked it's way up my throat when my foot slipped on the rotten wood of one of the boards, but Edik swung me to the side, keeping me from falling as the board collapsed. "Slow and steady. We're not far now."

I didn't speak, instead I prayed to myself. *Creator, let us get safely to the castle. Let me find my way back to my husbands.* A strange prickling sensation filled my head, but I shook it away as I took the final steps off of the bridge. Dina embraced me immediately, "You made it. We're just around the corner from the castle."

"Let's keep moving." I insisted.

We walked in silence, while I did my best not to gawk at the gorgeous scenery. Statues of various figures lined the paths, each one of them were wrapped in vines from years of neglect, but it only added to the mysterious beauty. The path was paved with blue stone, that glittered brightly underneath the two suns. To our left a hedge that easily stood eight feet tall took up the space, thorny roses protruded from it.

"What is that?" Duchess asked, motioning toward an opening in the hedge.

"That is the entrance to the Queen's Maze. Please do not go in there as there's no guarantee you will make it out." Edik explained, "The Maze holds the crowns many secrets. Only the royals and their most trusted confidants can enter and exit without harm"

"It's said there are creatures that live within that can smell the blood of trespassers." Kori added, his bright laugh cutting off the anxiety I'd felt at Edik's description. There were so many dangers in this world that we didn't even know to watch for. I'd never imagined it like this when Eumonia had described Undraland. Yet for every dangerous thing we came across ten things that were beautiful and magickal. Some part of me longed to explore this strange land, but I had a responsibility to get back to Wonderland. Back to my husbands. Back to Dina's daughter, Elsie.

I glanced to my friend, noting the pale cast to her usually vibrant mocha skin. She was not handling the travel in Undraland well. We needed to get her home as soon as possible.

Duchess gasped up ahead drawing my attention. As I came to her side I gasped as well. The Queen's castle towered above us, white and black marble shaped every inch of the huge palace. Vines had grown over half of the surface, but it only added to the mysterious beauty.

"Welcome to the Queen's Castle, ladies. Why don't we hurry up and get inside." Edik said.

The inside of the castle was homier than I expected. Soft, golden light flickered in sconces every few feet. Some kind of magick clearly kept them lit all this time, because it was clear to me the place was deserted. A heavy layer of dust coated every surface I'd come across. Yet the inside of the castle was almost as stunning as the outside. The whole place was decorated in blues, greens, and silvers. Glittering chandeliers hung in every room, paintings of former royalty hung down the hallway on either side, velvet curtains hung over stained-glass windows depicting everything from strange creatures to scenes of love and war. I could feel the magick that infused the entire place, pulsing like a heartbeat beneath my feet. A sense of comfort filled me unlike any I'd felt before. I couldn't deny the feeling of belonging that bloomed in my chest.

"It's beautiful." Dina said, as we stood at the entrance of a large bedroom. I felt guilty at my strange relaxation here. I could not stay. My husbands and our family were in Wonderland.

"Why don't you take this room? I'll get the one down the hall. You look like you need some rest." I suggested.

Dina didn't argue, hiding a yawn. Kori appeared, "I've got clean bedding for you both. Give me just a second to put it on." He said, pushing past us to enter the room. He was a flurry of motion as he stripped the king bed, and put on clean, white sheets. He topped it with a light grey duvet. "Enjoy. Queen Alice, have you selected your room? I'll do yours next."

"That one on the left, but please Kori, just call me Alice. You don't have to make our beds for us, we aren't incapable." I said.

"It's my honor to serve." He responded, dismissing my words to head to the room I'd indicated I would take.

"I'm going to explore for a while. I'll be back later." I told Dina before she entered her room, closing the door.

I wandered the halls for a while. Staring at every painting. It was odd to see the images of people that were so clearly my ancestors. I couldn't help but imagine a life where I had grown up with Lily inside these walls. Seeing my mother truly fulfilling her role as the White Queen. It wasn't hard to imagine. I found a staircase, taking the curving stairs down. The air grew thicker with magick, but I didn't stop. My entire body buzzed as I came into a large room. Only a golden well sat in the center. I ran my hand over the walls, checking for hidden doors. When nothing opened, I approached the well, electricity lifting from my skin and snapping in the air around me. I reached out, laying my hand on a well. I fell to my knees as power sizzled through my entire body. I couldn't move as electricity swirled around me. Before I could scream out, the world went dark.

"Hello, daughter." An echoing, but familiar voice filled my ears. My eyes snapped open, taking in the foggy space where I'd awakened. "Take your time. Absorbing the Queen's power may have left your body feeling sore."

The voice was right. My arms ached, even though I knew I wasn't conscious I could feel every pain in my body. I could also feel my magick, stronger and wilder than it had been before. "What do you mean, the Queen's power?" I asked, forcing myself to sit up.

"You have always been such a curious girl, Alice. Your mother did well in selecting your name." I couldn't find where the voice emanated from.

"Who are you?" I asked.

Fog parted a few feet ahead of me, revealing a silver glowing figure. It seemed feminine, but with the shifting light I couldn't make out any details. "You know who I am. Listen to your heart." I couldn't say it. If it were true... "Yes, Alice. I am the Creator."

"How?" That single word was filled with so much meaning. How was I here talking to the Creator? How had I ended up in Undraland? How did I get home? How did I save Wonderland?

"You are the end of a long line of Queens I have blessed. I cannot reach out on Earth, but you now dwell in the realm I created. The realm that I have gifted to your bloodline." The Creator explained. I opened my mouth to ask more questions, but she held up her hand, "Our time together is limited, please let me speak." I nodded, so she continued, "There is a sickness upon my world. One that has been festering for hundreds of years. It's caused by the one you know as the Queen of Hearts. Without my chosen Queen on the throne, managing the magick it has been allowed to spread, until all the creatures of my world suffer. I need you to heal Undraland. To take your place as the rightful Queen."

"I have to go home." I said, unable to stop myself.

A sense of sadness filled the Creator's words, "I know you see Earth as your home, and I promise that what you do here will ultimately lead you to your goals. But please, trust the path I lead you toward. Without you, Undraland will die. The creatures and people left here will suffer."

"What do I need to do?" I asked. I couldn't allow people to die if I could stop it. Just as I was responsible for Wonderland, I had some responsibility for Undraland as well.

"First, you must enter the maze. The answers you seek lie at its center." The warm approval in her voice filled me.

"But the Knights said it was dangerous." I said, nervously.

"When have you let danger stop you from anything, Alice? Do this task for me, and all that you desire shall be yours. The path will not be without pain but know that I am always watching over you." The Creator's form started to fade.

I rushed forward, "Are my husbands okay?" I rushed to ask.

A soft chuckle met my ears as the world swam, "I protect all my children, but especially those that belong to you."

I came awake to clammy hands shaking me, "Alice! Alice!" Duchess shouted, ignoring the way my magick seemed to snap out at her.

I sat up, nearly causing us to collide, "We've got to talk to the Knights."

"What the fuck is going on?" She snapped.

"I just talked to the Creator." I shout back at her as I rushed up the stairs. I had a mission; nothing was going to stop me now. Not when the Creator themselves had given me a task.

Chapter 8

Caterpillar

April 1ˢᵗ, 2159

The wind was needle like against my skin as I swung the bike around another curve dangerously fast. I'd found riding was the only thing that kept my mind off of killing everyone until I found Alice. I didn't realize how much Alice had changed my life until she was gone. Without a thought I'd slipped right back to my anti social ways. I'm sure if she was here I'd get an earful for how I had been behaving. The thought brought a small smile to my face, but it was bittersweet at best. With Cheshire's help I had forced myself to resume my duties alongside Eumonia as the leaders of Wonderland. I'd jumped on the bike as soon as Eumonia and I had finished a meeting with the magick users over the strange earthquakes that had started over the last few days. It was just another sign that the Queen of Hearts was up to something, but Eumonia wasn't sure so we called on the magick users of Wonderland to do whatever they could to protect the city from damage. Two buildings had already partially crumbled, one person had been killed. Even one life lost was too many. Things were supposed to be better for Wonderland under my hand. Somehow they only seemed to be getting worse.

I sighed as our building came into view. I didn't want to talk to Alcinda, but I promised her we would sit down today. She was insistent on a family meal. I couldn't deny her, with the dark bags that had taken residence under her eyes since Alice's disappearance. I trudged to her apartment, helmet still under my arm. Before I could even knock on the door, it swung open, a grinning Cheshire greeting me, "Welcome back, Bossman. How was the ride?"

The mischief that gleamed in his eyes set me on edge, but I responded, "Finc. Is everyone already here?"

He nodded before leading me inside. While the apartments all had a similar lay out, each one was vastly different. Alcinda's was decorated in plush whites and golds with hints of green. It was tasteful and definitely fit the older woman well. As we entered the dining room I stiffened when an unfamiliar man greeted me, "Caterpillar, I'm Henry Tinniel. March and Lewis' father."

March had told me that he'd met his biological father, but I hadn't been told he'd be joining us tonight. I glanced to Lewis, who was playing with a stuffed duck and lion next to Alcinda, "Do you plan to take Lewis?" Every eye in the room turned to me, but I didn't care. This man had abandoned both of his sons. I wanted to know exactly what his intentions were.

"I want to be in his life, as his father, but I'm not selfish. He's clearly been given a wonderful life here. He's already attached to Alcinda. I wouldn't snatch him away from that." Henry said.

I nodded, "Talk to Rab about getting you set up in one of the smaller apartment's downstairs. You should be nearby." His eyes widened, but I changed the subject before he could respond, "Aren't we supposed to be having dinner?"

Alcinda stood, ruffling Lewis' hair before exiting the room. When she returned she carried a huge pot. She sat it in the center of the table, "This was Alice's favorite when she was a little girl."

I couldn't help the tension in my body as she mentioned my wife. My eyes drifted to Eumonia, only to find her already looking at me. She gave me a small nod. An acknowledgement of the pain I carried. I couldn't stand to look at her face for too long. It was too similar to Alice's face, the button nose, the wide crystal blue eyes and full lips. There was differences between them. Anyone here could tell the difference with ease. Eumonia carried herself differently, as if her age was a weight dragging her down. She was also quieter, more reserved. All that looking at her did for me was remind me of how I had failed the only woman I loved.

Everyone dug into the chili Alcinda had made. I spooned food into my mouth quickly to avoid the conversations that were taking place around me. I didn't want to be a part of them. Thankfully the chili was the best I'd ever had. Thick, meaty with tons of fresh tomatoes. Even the scent was heavenly.

"Actually, I never intended to have another child." Alcinda said, drawing my attention.

"Really?" I asked, curious to hear more about how Alice had come to be.

"I mean... It was irresponsible to have Lily considering that I was always being hunted by Penthea, but Charles and I were desperate to feel like a normal family. I told him I wouldn't have any more kids until Wonderland was safe." She trailed off for a moment, a far away look in her eyes, "When Lily was five I had a vision, I saw Alice as an adult... In fact I saw the moment she shot my sister." Everyone at the table was silent at that admission. I had no idea that she'd had such a detailed vision about Alice before she'd even been conceived. It certainly made more of her choices make sense. "Charles and I battled for months about it. He didn't want to bring a child into the world just because I had a vision. Ultimately, I won. And we gave Alice the best life we could without the pressure of what my vision had shown."

"You're saying I could have been an only child?" Lily asked. The joke caused me to snort, helping to relieve the tension that had built at the table.

"Seeing is the hardest gift to manage. We want to change the lives of the people we love and change the future. Sometimes we are afforded that ability, but more often we are forced to watch the events unfold powerlessly." Eumonia said.

"Magick can be a blessing or a curse. It all depends on how you look at it and how we choose to use our abilities." Henry chimed in, "We've all seen the devasting effects of a magick user using their ability to do evil. I believe that together, using our abilities for good everything will work out in the end."

"The Creator always has a plan." Eumonia agreed, "I know we're all feeling defeated after our loss at the wedding, but I know Alice is still out there working to get back to us. We aren't going to let the Queen of Hearts beat us."

Shouts of agreement flooded the table, but I sat in silence. What costs would the people I love have to pay? As I looked to Rab, I knew the price would be higher than any of us wanted to imagine. It always was.

Chapter 9

Alice

April 2ⁿᵈ, 2159

It hadn't taken much to convince the Knights that we had to enter the maze. Even if they were hesitant, whatever had happened had solidified in their mind that I was their Queen. It didn't matter if I continued to deny it, they weren't budging. Dina and Duchess had been harder to convince. I had considered letting them stay in the castle, but splitting the group up in an unfamiliar land wasn't an option. Two non-magick users weren't safe anywhere in Undraland right now. The Knights wouldn't let me enter the maze alone, so the girls had to join us. As I heaved a heavy bag over my shoulders I wished for the tenth time that the guys were with me. Being on this journey without them was harder than I wanted to admit. I loved Dina, but I couldn't talk to her about all the things I was learning about myself. I couldn't talk about the way my magick now flowed under my skin like water, just waiting to be used. Duchess was worse. She didn't want to hear about any magick at all.

"Are you ready?" Edik's voice startled me out of my thoughts. I nodded, following him from the room. Ledger, Kori, Duchess, and Dina all waited on us, bags on their backs. Weapons were strapped across every available surface of their bodies. Twin axes hung on either side of Duchess' hips. Dina had something that looked like a crossbow hanging off her shoulder.

I was glad they'd taken the time to arm themselves. We had no idea what we would find inside the maze. The Knights were willing to go in only because of the vision I'd been shown. Even now I could feel their tension. We left the castle in silence, stepping out into the bright sun. I'd dressed in thin blue pants and a simple white shirt. My bag had thicker clothes for the cold nights, but Edik had prepared me that the maze would be hours of walking in the heat.

"Are you sure we should do this?" Dina asked as the maze came into view.

"If the Creator has asked it of her, she cannot say no. One way or another Alice will enter the maze and fulfill the Creator's request." Ledger's voice was harsh, likely from misuse. He was eerily quiet most of the time, what little he did say was damn near feral.

Duchess scoffed but said nothing. I'd already heard her opinion on the Creator's request. She didn't truly believe the Creator existed, and even if they did, she didn't like them. I understood it. Her mother had tortured her for years, only for her to be kidnapped by a crazy immortal woman and tortured again. Duchess was angry at the world for valid reasons. I hoped that one day she healed, but first I had to get her back home.

"Let's fucking do this." I said, stepping my foot into the maze. Hesitation wouldn't get me back to my husbands or help the Creator.

As soon as the last person stepped into the maze the ground shook around us, as if the world itself had felt our entrance and was warning us to run while we still had the chance. I turned, reconsidering my decision, only to find that our only way out had closed behind us. We were officially trapped inside the maze.

"Oh great. That's a good sign." Duchess snapped, before she began to stomp off. Before she could go far, Ledger swept her off her feet.

She screamed and beat against his armor as he tossed her over his shoulder, "Too much danger to run off. When you decide to behave I'll sit you down."

"You Creator damned fucking beast. Let me go." She screeched in response.

Edik ignored her continued cursing, "We have to move forward."

I nodded. I stared at the path head, the dirt road was nothing special. The hedges nearly blocked out the suns from our current position. The only way forward was through the maze.

We walked for hours, the only conversation was the sounds of Duchess' complaints and Ledger's grunts of annoyance. He'd finally set her down, but she'd made it her mission to ensure he suffered through the rest of the maze.

When I noticed a white rose standing out starkly from the rest of the hedge I cursed, "That's the sixth time we've passed that. We're just moving in circles."

I dropped my backpack in frustration. Resting my hands on my knees while I heaved, anxiety coursed through my body. My magick was responding, burning underneath my skin. It met my panic in a storm, bursting out of me with a scream. Instead of shots of electricity, silver lightning appeared before me. In a shaky line, pointing straight before it disappeared around a corner.

"Alice... are you okay?" Dina asked, a hand resting on my shoulder.

I couldn't respond, staring at the line of buzzing electricity that ran ahead of us.

"It's a path. We should follow it." Edik observed. "Can you maintain it?"

"I don't even know how I did that." I snapped.

"We follow it. Maybe it will at least lead us out of the loop." Kori said.

I let them lead the way, panting and exhausted as every inch of my skin itched as if I'd been badly sun burnt. Yet my magick felt as strong as ever. My emotions were out of control. I hadn't dealt with these feelings since I was a teenager. I had no idea why I felt so… unstable. We walked until we began to hear rustling ahead. Edik stopped everyone, moving slowly. When a shiny white creature that resembled a cat jumped from one of the bushes, Kori screamed, "Shadelumes. Everyone cover your ears."

I didn't have a chance to do as he said before another shimmering cat appeared before me. When it opened its mouth and spoke I nearly fainted, "A lost Queen. Disgraced Knights. Someone smells of secrets." Its head turned at an unnatural angle, as it took a deep breath, "Basha will assist you, lost Queen, for our Creator has commanded it. But you will owe a favor to the Shadelumes."

I swallowed hard, barely comprehending its words, "Th-thank you."

The cat grinned, showing two sets of deadly fangs, "We are indebted to the Lyon line. Tell your party they will be safe from our riddles for now."

I turned, waving at everyone who was covering their ears. Edik cautiously stood, "They are going to help us." I explained.

He was still for a long moment, and once again I wished the Knights would remove their helmets so I could read their faces. Finally, he nodded, "I trust your judgement."

Some part of me wanted to tell him not to. Some part of me was just a lost girl in a land she didn't know, playing pretend while my friends lives hung in the balance. From the moment I'd opened my eyes in Undraland, I'd been unsure. Instead of expressing any of that I turned back to Basha, "I'm looking for something."

"I know what you seek, lost Queen. But I cannot take you all the way. I will guide you safely nearby so that you may rest overnight." She responded. Her mouth didn't exactly move, and I finally realized that I was hearing her words in my mind.

Basha kept her promise. As the two suns set, darkness crept through the maze throwing strange shadows she led us to a small clearing. Only two lanterns, and the shimmering fur of Basha lit the small area. The Knights efficiently set up our camp, ensuring everyone had somewhere to sleep. We ate on dried meat and fruit that we'd all packed in our bags. No one spoke.

"What exactly is a Shadelume?" Dina finally asked, unable to keep her eyes from Basha.

"They look like shiny cats." Duchess said.

Basha made a snorting sound, "The human girl said the same thing when she entered Undraland all those years ago. We do bare some resemblance to the cats of Earth, but the Creator gave us psychic magick and long lives."

"Psychic magick?" I asked.

"They can drive you mad." Edik explained, "In fact, it's one of their favorite past times."

Basha looked from her licking her paw, "Do you know that we were once hunted and drained by members of the Red King's guard for our magick? The Shadelumes are a proud race. We will not be prey for mere mortals."

"I'm sorry your people went through that. We won't harm you." I said.

Basha gave me a solemn nod before she returned to her grooming, and I laid back on my sleeping bag. The stars here were nothing like the ones on Earth, instead of white, yellow, or blue they shined in purples and reds. The moon was similar enough, bigger and brighter, but as I stared into it I felt some comfort. Every step I'd taken in Undraland brought me closer to getting home, I could feel something building. Anticipation and something more. Something that would change all of our lives.

I glanced around, seeing that everyone had fallen asleep. From the depths of my pocket I pulled out a folded photo. I stared down at it, tears dripping onto the glossy surface. I was standing in the center of the picture wearing simple work out gear, my hair up in a ponytail. I was loosely holding a dagger. Cheshire was standing next to me, throwing a peace sign, his tongue was out showing his piercing, and his nose was slightly scrunched. Caterpillar was standing behind me, a small smirk playing across his features, as he wrapped an arm around my waist. Hatter was gripping one of my hands, while his other arm was thrown around March's shoulders. I missed them so much. Lily had snapped the photo after our first work out in our own gym. She had laughed when she'd snapped this photo, because they guys argued over who should stand where. I gently wiped the wetness off the picture and tucked it back into my pocket, glancing toward Dina's sleeping form. She was shivering slightly, so I crawled over and snuggled against her back.

At least I wasn't completely alone. Without Dina, Duchess, and the Knights I don't know that I would have made it this far.

Chapter 10

April 4th, 2159

We all awoke with the suns, eating our simple food again, and returned to our walk once again. When we arrived at a fork in the road, Basha stepped before me, "Queen Alice, I am unable to lead you any further. The road ahead is only for a queen and her people to walk. You will meet no other creatures within this section of the maze but know that there are still dangers. This maze was created to protect the royal secrets. They have been buried for many years. Undraland will not give those secrets up without bloodshed." With those final words, she disappeared back into the hedges.

I glanced toward my small group, Dina and Duchess had both paled, "You can wait here. Maybe she'll come back and lead you out of the maze." I offered.

"No." Ledger commanded from the back of the group.

I raised an eyebrow at his tone, "I can handle the maze from here alone."

"We are not leaving you, because of the spoiled brat and the human." He growled.

Before I could respond, Edik put up his hands, "He's right, Alice. We cannot leave you. Please, just allow us to protect the three of you the rest of the way."

I looked between Edik and Ledger for a long moment, weighing their words. I didn't know this land the way they did. Going forward alone wasn't ideal. I sighed, "Everyone stay behind me. If we have to fight, you will prioritize their lives over mine. Is that understood?"

Edik gave me a sharp nod. I took a steadying breath before I turned back to the fork in the maze. Basha hadn't told us which way to go, but somehow, I knew. I could feel something calling to me. I followed the left path as it curved and widened.

Hours passed, my legs becoming leaden as we continue to tread through the maze. The only sounds were our breathing and the occasional clink of the Knight's armor. I'd become comfortable with our silence since we started to journey together. Yet it only made me miss my husbands more. Cheshire would fill the silence with his jokes, Caterpillar wouldn't let me out of his sight, Hatter and March would be racing and keeping us all entertained. As my thoughts drifted, the sky darkened.

I glanced up, finding that the maze here was overgrown. The suns couldn't penetrate the deep green growth. I slowed to a stop as my magick began to buzz under my skin. Seconds later, the ground beneath our feet began to melt our boots sticking into the strange liquid that had appeared. I almost fell forward, but Edik grabbed an arm around my middle, "Take your shoes off!" He shouted in my ear. Edik held me up, as I ripped my feet from my shoes. Once I was free, he launched me several feet into the air. I tangled my fingers into the hedges, ignoring the cuts that opened on my hands. I swung my body, using my momentum to swing myself further down the hedge. Eventually, I dropped onto hard dirt, panting. My hands were bleeding profusely from the cuts, but I turned back watching as Ledger and Kori threw Duchess toward me. I managed to catch her inches before she would have fallen into the strange soft dirt. Edik dropped to the ground next to me, Dina jumping down from his back. Once Kori and Ledger made it across we all stood, panting and bleeding.

"We need to keep moving. The maze is starting to fight back." Edik commanded. No one argued, too shaken by our close call to say anything.

I could tell we were reaching our destination. My magick was haywire, electricity crackling under my skin and in the air around me.

"You all need to stay a few feet back." I said as we took a turn that opened into a large circular garden.

The smell of roses was the first thing to hit me. Sickly sweetness hanging in the air, nearly choking me out. The roses bloomed in colors I'd never seen before, shades of blue and green that were unnatural. I watched as Dina approached one, running her fingers gently over the leaves. Ledger carefully plucked several roses, tucking them into the bag he kept around his waist. He'd done this several times throughout our journey, but I didn't have the courage to ask what he used the plants for.

Duchess was pale when I turned to her, it didn't take long for me to realize why. There were several statues throughout the garden, but the one she stared at was nearly identical to her father. I approached her, reading the plaque that had been placed at the statue's feet, "The Red King, also known as Mered Rose, ruled over Undraland for nearly two hundred years after his wife Bethandra Lyon was killed. His magick was vast, but unfortunately slowly drove him insane. Alice Liddell, a human girl from Earth, freed Undraland of his rule on July 4th, 1865, with the help of magick user Lewis Carroll." Duchess sniffed, and I noticed a single tear running down her face. We didn't speak as I wrapped an arm around her. I knew she was grieving her father's death.

She pulled away, wiping tears from her face, "I'm fine."

"I know." I nodded, moving to read a different statue's plaque. I explored for a long time, learning more and more about the royalty that had existed in Undraland before Eumonia. When I came to the final statue in the center of the maze, there was no plaque. It wore the same armor as the Knights, but it was covered in vines and roses. As I glanced to the sword it held my magick reacted, arcing toward it. I couldn't stop myself from stepping forward, wrapping my fingers around the hilt. With little effort the sword came free, glowing with silver starlight as I held it aloft. I gasped as it morphed from a great sword to a thin curved blade. It fit perfectly in my grip as if it had been made especially for me. While I'd always been partial to daggers, this blade called to my magick.

I was so enraptured by the sword I didn't notice that the statue I'd taken it from had come to life. When its green, vine coated hand wrapped around my arm, I screamed. I plunged my blade into the soft spot on its shoulder, not expecting blood to squirt from the wound. A deep grunt responded. I pulled my sword away in a panic, stumbling back. The statue chased after me, closing the small space I made in seconds.

The armored statue reached up, removing its helmet, and I found myself staring into the strange swirling silver eyes of a giant man. His dark skin was smooth, making it impossible to tell his age. Long black locs, edged in green fell to his shoulders.

I heard the clink of armor, turning to find that Edik, Ledger, and Kori had all fallen to their knees behind me. Dina and Duchess stood shocked behind them.

"You are not Eumonia Lyon, as much as you may favor her." The Knight said, his voice deep rumbling through me due to his closeness.

"I am Alice Young. Eumonia is one of my ancestors." I explained, too taken aback by his appearance to do anything but respond. "I stabbed you... Are you okay?"

He glanced toward the spot on his shoulder, "The Vorporal sword cannot harm any who are loyal to the crown."

"The Vorporal Sword?" I questioned, glancing back to the glowing blade still clutched in my right hand.

His eyebrows knit together as he stared at me. My magick responded to my feelings, arcing toward him. When it made contact, he didn't react like he'd been electrocuted. Instead, he let out a gasp, reaching for me. His lips crashed into mine as silver and green flared around us. Finally, I pulled away, pushing him back with a little force. "I'm married!" I snapped, "What the fuck?"

"Apologies, Queen Alice, but you are my heartmate." He responded. My confusion must have been clear on my face, "Heartmates are connections made by the Creator. Our magick and souls are linked and aligned for the greater purpose of Undraland."

"Of course they are." Duchess snicked behind me, "Alice gets all the fine-looking men."

I sent her a glare. "Like I said, I'm married. The Creator sent me here to get something."

"More like someone." Dina added.

The strange Knight finally noticed the men kneeling at my back, skirting around me to address them, "Rise brothers. You've done well. Tell me of what has happened while I slept."

Edik spoke first, "It has been over one hundred and fifty years, my King. The curse still ravages the land. I awoke three years ago; Ledger and Kori have awoken since. We found the young Queen roaming with her friends. She came from Earth and is seeking a way home."

"Who is this man?" I asked, finally annoyed with their disregard.

"I am Wyth, leader of the Emerald Knights, advisor to the Queen of Undraland. The first of my title, the Emerald King." He responded, proudly.

"Wyth..." I repeated, trailing off. I did feel some strange attraction to him, yet guilt for betraying my husbands overrode whatever connection the Creator had created between us. "Can you get me home?"

"You're the one with a portaller." He responded, "Ask her to return you to your world."

When he nodded to Duchess, my world spun. Her eyes told me the truth. She'd known. Known that at any moment, she could have taken us home. This entire journey... Pointless.

PART TWO:

GOLDEN DUCHESS

Chapter 11

Hatter

April 7th, 2159

"We get in and out. Two teams, silent and deadly. Is everyone clear on that?" Caterpillar barked. This anonymous tip we'd received about a Red Party hide out had come in two days ago, and we had rushed to put together an infiltration plan. I knew Caterpillar had some hope that we might be able to find the Queen of Hearts. I didn't think we would. She's always been a step ahead of us, even once we ended her spying through Ilaria. The woman was smart and had clearly been planning her Wonderland takeover of longer than most of us had been alive if Eumonia was to be believed. "Sammy, Cheshire, Lily, and Eumonia, you're with me. Patrick, March, Idalia, and Rab, you're with Hatter. We leave out in ten minutes."

I rolled my shoulders as I headed down to the garage. What had once been my favorite place in our home now brought me sadness. The Hummer was totaled months ago, but I still hadn't found another vehicle. The motorcycles worked, and I had learned to enjoy riding them, but it was nothing like the Hummer. I shook my head, compared to Alice's disappearance the Hummer meant nothing. I had hope that my wife was somewhere close by, that we might find her being held by the Red Party. Yet something told me that wasn't true. If Alice was somewhere that she could escape from, she would have made her way back by now.

"You okay?" Cheshire asked, causing me to drop the helmet I'd just picked up.

"Creator damned Cat." I muttered, before sighing, "Yeah man, I'm fine."

"It's okay if you aren't, you know. None of us are doing the best, we're a mess without her." He said.

"I don't need you to be my therapist, Cheshire. My father did that enough when I was a kid." I blew him off. I didn't need to talk about my feelings, I needed to find Alice. I needed answers.

"Don't do anything reckless." He responded, before pulling a helmet over his head and mounting his bike. Before I could respond, everyone filed into the garage, effectively ending our conversation. I wasn't the impulsive one, why would Cheshire think differently? What sign had he seen that made him fear what I would do next? Had Alcinda seen something... I shook my head. It didn't matter. We were going into a mission. One that might shed light on what had happened to Alice. I needed answers. I needed my wife back.

The house we arrived at was brightly lit, though there was no movement to be seen through the windows. We had parked our cars and bikes two streets over, ensuring that no one would hear us coming. I didn't know if that truly mattered, considering how little we knew about the magick users that were on the Queen of Hearts side.

I guided my small group to the back door. I reached for my lock picking set, but Idalia reached for the knob, finding it unlocked. She threw me a concerned glance, but I motioned for all of us to enter. The house was eerily quiet, a lingering scent of disinfectant and something sharp burned my nose as we rounded the corner. A bang from behind us followed by a masculine grunt had me spinning around. My eyes couldn't focus because of the smoke that had filled the hallway. I scrambled for the gun at my hip, stumbling toward a door to get away from the smoke. There were sounds of fighting, but I couldn't see well enough to help my team. I threw open a nearby door, eyes watering, darkness surrounding me. The door I'd just entered slammed shut behind me, and a masculine laugh filled the room.

"Just my luck, I can finally exact my revenge." Jabberwocky's distinct accent filled the room. "I wondered when I'd run into you. Your little boy toy took my arm, I wonder how he'll feel when I take your life?"

"I've been wanting a shot at you ever since you hurt my wife." I growled. Alice's scars flashed through my mind. Suddenly the pain of my burning eyes and the darkness didn't matter. I dropped into a defensive stance, my gun raised, ears open to any tiny sound in the room. When the quiet whoosh of clothes moving met my ears, I pivoted pulling the trigger of my gun without hesitation. I heard the bullet hit metal, but Jabberwocky grunted.

I wasn't prepared for my legs to be swept out from under me. I rolled, seconds before something thunked against the ground, narrowly avoiding whatever weapon he wielded. A kick to my ribs stopped me from getting up, but I grabbed his leg, yanking with all my might until his body collapsed on the ground as well.

We grappled, grunts and the sound of punches landing were all that filled the room. When a sharp pain sliced through my leg I knew I was in trouble. Hot liquid ran down my leg. Before I could get away and attend to the wound Jabberwocky managed to get on top of me, his fist slamming into my face. The crack of my nose breaking deafened me.

Jabberwocky was laughing as he pummeled me, my arms pinned under his knees. For the first time in my life, I was losing a fight. True fear seized my chest. This psychopath wanted me dead, and he had the upper hand. When a cold blade touched my throat, I sent a prayer to the Creator. *I know I haven't prayed in a while, but please. I can't protect Alice if I die today. March has lost enough. Give me a way out.*

Seconds later light flooded the room, burning my already injured eyes. Jabberwocky didn't stop, plunging a knife into my chest. Pain shot through my body. A shrill and haunting sound rang through my ears. Jabberwocky hissed, standing and abandoning me as March appeared. I blinked, shocked to see that he was coated in blood. A vicious snarl on his beautiful face, but the most surprising part was that the strange haunting sound was coming from his lips. He was haloed in an indigo light, similar to Alice's glow.

My magick seemed to respond to his, white flowing into my fingertips. A voice spoke into my mind, *"Heal yourself, child of Earth. For you are one of the Queen's Knights."* I didn't hesitate to follow its command, laying my glowing hand over my own chest. Burning pain ripped through my body, but when I pulled away the worst of the stab wound was closed. My body was still beaten, blood running down almost every inch of my skin, but I could tell none of my injuries were life-threatening now. I tried to stand, to go to March who was locked in combat with Jabberwocky, but I collapsed unable to move.

I was forced to watch as Jabberwocky sliced his knife across March's face. Rage lit inside me, but I could do nothing. The people I loved had been hurt by this man, were in danger every waking moment, and I was unable to do anything to protect them when they needed it the most. Fear warred with helplessness in my chest my heart pounding against my ribcage violently.

When March parried a blow, sinking the curved dagger I'd given him for Christmas into Jabberwocky's gut I cheered. "Kick his fucking ass, March."

Jabberwocky spit blood, his body was shaking with his rage, but March didn't react at all. Instead, he raised his blade again, and said, "No one hurts my fucking husband." With one clean arc, Jabberwocky's head rolled off his shoulders landing inches from my feet.

March rushed to my side, "Are you o-okay?"

"I've been beaten to a pulp, had a strange voice speak in my head, and my amazing husband just saved my life like the badass he is... I'm... I'm exhausted, Maxton." That was all I could say.

"Me too, Hayden, me too." He responded as he helped me to my feet. "B-but you know what, its nice that the shoe is on the other foot for once."

"Huh?"

"Everyone is always saving me. It's nice to be the hero for once." March explained.

I thought for a moment, before the truth tumbled from my lips, "In a way you've always been my hero. I don't know anyone else that could have gone through everything that you have and maintained any sanity."

"I wouldn't say I'm completely s-sane." He joked.

"I'm being serious, March. You are strong, intelligent, and handsome. You aren't lesser than anyone. Honestly... You're probably the best of us all, because you have a truly kind heart."

"I just cut off a man's head." March pointed out.

"He deserved it." I kissed his temple as we limped out of the house, "I love you so much."

"I love you too, Hayden... And thank you. For always being there for me. I couldn't have done it all without you."

Chapter 12

Alice

April 10ᵗʰ, 2159

I paced in the mostly dark bedroom, ignoring the suns that were rising over the castle grounds. I'd been unsettled for days. Duchess' lies, Wyth's appearance and strange behavior... I hadn't slept properly either. Yet, my magick seemed unaffected. Even that added to my stress. Why had my magick changed so much in Undraland? Why did the Creator send me to retrieve the Vorporal Sword and the Emerald King? Who just so happened to have some strange, romantic connection to me... The Creator hadn't shown themselves again. I had no answers, and my questions seemed to grow with each passing moment.

I had no way to confirm if what the King said was true. Yet... I had felt something. Something similar to how I'd felt the first time the guys and I had really bonded. As if just being in their presence was... right. It was wrong though, I couldn't feel something for Wyth while I was an entire world away from the men, I'd just made vows to.

"Stress will kill even a Queen of your magnitude." Wyth's voice filled the room pulling me into the present.

I whirled around, taking in his appearance. He was taller than Caterpillar easily, probably approaching seven feet so I had to crane my neck to meet his strange eyes. He'd chopped off his long locs, instead sporting a stylish shaved look. The scars that ran over his arms and crept toward his face did nothing to take away from his looks. I couldn't deny that he was attractive. That I felt something when I looked at him. More than lust. "How did you get those?" I asked, ignoring his comment.

"I defeated the Bandersnatch. It's head still hangs in the hallway of Kings if you'd like to see." He responded proudly.

"I have no idea what that is, but I don't think I want to see it's severed head." I said, before sighing. "You didn't come here to discuss that. What can I do for you?"

"I wish you wouldn't ask it like that. There are many things that I'd like for you to do for me, that I'm sure your... husbands would not be pleased by." He rumbled. He moved closer as he spoke, his hands now inches from touching my cheek, "I never thought I'd be turned on by knife wounds, but the closest you've been to me is when you shoved the Vorporal sword into my shoulder."

I swallowed, "I'm sorry. I know... No honestly, I don't know what you're feeling. I don't understand any of this."

He smoothed the hair away from my face, "We have all the time in the world, Alice. Just give me a chance."

"And what would you expect me to do? I am married... To four men." I back away, returning to my pacing.

"What's one more husband?" He countered, before pulling me to a stop, "Do you not think they would like me?"

"I don't know you well enough to know that." I knew I was avoiding getting closer to him. I didn't want to betray my men, but Wyth was temptation personified. I could fall for him.

"We can change that. Give me a chance to know you, to learn you. I am an open book to you and you alone. Anything you ask me I will answer. Maybe you'll figure out that the Creator doesn't make mistakes." Wyth said, all while his thumb traced over my collarbone.

I couldn't deny the way my body reacted to him. I wanted him, and it had been weeks since I'd even thought about sex. My body was coming alive under his touch, but guilt rose with it. "I still need to go home. Whatever this is doesn't change that."

He nodded, stepping away. I could see the heat in his eyes, but he said, "I will not stand in your way of returning to Earth. On that subject, have you spoken to Duchess?"

I shook my head, "I haven't been able to look at her without rage. Why would she keep me trapped here if she could take us home at any time?"

"You should ask her that." Wyth said, before bowing at the waist, "I must return to my Knights, but I hope you'll join me for dinner tonight."

I nodded, not trusting what I might say. The urge to ask him to stay and distract me from my spinning thoughts turned my tongue to lead. Instead, I planted my feet, waiting until the sound of his footsteps no longer echoed down the hall.

I stared out the window for a long time, watching as the suns bathed the maze in golden light. I noticed Basha lurking near the entrance, her white and purple fur shimmering brightly. When she glanced up, meeting my eyes I gave her a nod that she returned. I felt an odd sort of kinship with the Shadelume. As I continued to watch the castle grounds, I noticed Duchess exit the castle. It was the first time I'd seen her since I'd woken Wyth and retrieved the Vorporal sword. Even from here I could see the tension in her shoulders as she walked through the small gardens.

I turned away from the window, as my magick responded to my complicated emotions. Electricity snapped around me, but I took a deep breath, willing it to return to me. Once it had passed, I slipped into the attached bathroom, filling the large golden tub with steaming hot water. Something I'd found out I could thank Kori for. His magick involved some sort of water manipulation, so he'd been the one to ensure all the plumbing was working. As I climbed in, I let the water wash away all of my stress.

Duchess sat with her head held high as I entered the office Wyth had declared to be mine. It was a beautiful room, mostly taken up by two large couches made of a soft, green material and a grand wooden desk that had carvings of a tree on the front. I closed the door, ensuring our privacy before taking the seat across from her. We stared at each other for a long time, no words were passed between us, yet when I opened my mouth to speak I had a new understanding, "You didn't know until she took you."

Duchess swallowed hard, and nodded. Her voice was shaky when she finally spoke, "I... I've only managed to open a portal once..." A tear rolled down her face, "When she killed my father. I was so upset, my magick responded. I would have gotten away... could have escaped, but... She's just better than I am."

"Why didn't you tell me when we got here? Why keep it to yourself as we struggled to find a way home?" I asked.

"Because I don't know that I can control it!" She snapped, her composure breaking completely, "Fuck. You think I want to be stuck here away from home, knowing that I should have the power to take us all back, but I just... can't. You think I haven't tried?"

"I can help." I said, an idea finally formed in my mind. "I can power you up, you can use me like a battery to open a portal home."

Duchess stared at me for a long moment, before bursting into hysterical laughter. I sat in stunned silence until she finally caught her breath, "Alice... You can't be serious. That's exactly what the Queen of Hearts wants!"

Fuck. I knew she was right but… I needed to find a way home more than I cared about what the Queen of Hearts might do. Every moment I was away was another day I couldn't protect Wonderland, "We may have to risk it."

"How can you say that after she stranded us here. She knew this would be your play." She argued.

I let the magick that was building in my chest begin to fill my skin, I breathed in deeply as I began to glow. My hair lifted from the electricity that rushed through my body, "Then she miscalculated, Duchess. I am more powerful than ever." Her eyes were wide as I slowly pulled the magick back into my body. The glow didn't fade completely, but I felt less tense. My magick was taking a huge toll on my body when I wasn't using it. At this point I believed it was likely due to whatever part of me was human. Eventually, I'd address that problem, but first I needed to get back home.

"When do you want to begin?" Duchess sighed. Defeat painted across her face and the slump of her shoulders.

"Whenever you're ready." I said.

"Might as well try it now." She stood, "Outside."

Duchess slumped to the ground, sweat pouring off of her, "I can't do it. I'm too weak."

"Stop saying that. Magick is hard to control, and you've only known about yours for a few weeks. It's going to take time." I said as I scuffed my shoe over a black mark on the ground. Every time Duchess' magick came out, and she reached into me to power herself up. Unfortunately, the moment she did whatever portal she conjured just imploded into black dust.

"Sorry to interrupt ladies," Wyth said as he approached, "I'm here to steal Alice away for dinner."

Edik approached Duchess, "You look tired. Whatever you're trying is draining you. Go inside and rest."

She stared up at the Knight for a long moment, before allowing him to help her off the ground. Once they were out of earshot, I glanced at Wyth with a raised brow, "That was interesting."

"Edik is a good man. He doesn't like to see anyone in pain." He waved me off, but I had a feeling it was more than that. The look on her face as he'd approached her had been... softer than she usually was. Something vulnerable and new was blooming in my cousin and I was excited for her. "Are you ready for dinner?"

I nodded, and allowed him to lead me inside, "I should change." I said suddenly as I glanced down at my white pants that were covered in black dust.

"You are a warrior Queen, I do not expect you to be anything else." He said as he opened an unfamiliar door. We stepped into a small room that held only a table for four and shelves full of strange carvings and artifacts I'd never seen before, "This is the Queen's private dining room. I thought you'd prefer it to the formal dining room."

"It's very cozy." I said as I ran my fingers over the closest shelf. One of the carvings caught my eye. It looked just like Sporekin, the details were insanely well done. "Who did these?"

"Eumonia's father, Demyan. He used every free moment craving the creatures of Undraland." Wyth explained as he came up behind me. I could feel the warmth of him through my clothes. I turned and found that I was staring at his broad chest. I glanced up meeting his swirling, silver eyes, "Can I kiss you again?"

I nodded, not trusting my voice. He bent down, pressing his lips to mine, gently at first, and then more roughly. Our tongues explored each other, and I moaned when his hands gripped my hips, roughly lifting me. Just as I was getting lost in the passion of our exchange, a small squeak drew my attention away. I drew away panting and noticed a small set of glowing blue eyes under the edge of the bookshelf I'd just been standing before. I stood, moving to kneel before the tiny creature, but Wyth laid a hand on my shoulder, "Not all things in Undraland are as kind as they may appear."

I shrugged his hand off, holding my hand out before the eyes, "Come here, baby. We won't hurt you." I sat completely still, waiting with bated breath for the creature to reveal itself. Finally, a tiny ball of glowing white fluff slipped out, sniffing my hand cautiously.

"Fuck. It's a baby Shadelume. Do not touch it. Its mother will strip the skin from your bones." Wyth sounded panic as he spoke, but I just rolled my eyes as the baby Shadelume curled up in my arms.

"It's just a baby. I'm sure Basha will understand. I'll go give it back to her." I turned on my heel, heading for the front of the maze where I'd seen Basha earlier in the day.

"Are we just going to ignore what just happened?" Wyth hollered as he ran after me, "How can you keep denying that you feel something from me?"

I walked faster at first, until I realized that I was literally running away from my problems. That wasn't who I was, so I stopped myself, taking a steadying breath. I turned, gently holding the baby Shadelume to my chest, "Because it feels like I'm cheating on my husbands! Because they probably think I'm dead, and I'm literally living in a castle and replacing them with you because of... magick? Or whatever the fuck a heartmate is."

"I'd never ask you not to be with them." He responded, "But I deserve a chance with you. A real one. Not guilty moments that you regret."

Before I could respond, Basha appeared on my shoulder, her claws digging into my skin, "I had wondered where little Nova had wandered off to," She spoke, before inclining her head to Wyth, "Emerald King. It's been many years."

Nova curled deeper into my arms, purring loudly. Basha leaned down, resting their foreheads together. A purple glow passed between them, before Basha jumped down from my shoulder, "It seems my daughter has chosen the life of a companion. You will treat her well, Queen or I will ensure that you find out why your heartmate fears my kind so much."

Wyth cringed as Basha twined herself between his legs, "She is far too young to leave you." I argued.

"We do not age as you do. She has told me that she wishes to be at your side. You will not dishonor her sacrifice. She could have been the next Queen." Basha snapped.

I stared down at Nova, her glowing blue eyes entrancing me. Some strange understanding passed through me, so I nodded, "Thank you, Basha. I will care for her."

Basha inclined her head, before disappearing from sight as if she'd never been there. I looked at Wyth, noting the tension in his body. I sighed, "I'm sorry. None of this is your fault... I just don't know how to deal with all these new revelations. A couple months ago, I was the leader of a normal, human city. Sure I had magick, but my primary focus was taking care of my people and getting time with the men I loved. Now, I'm supposed to be Queen of an entire world. The chosen of the Creator. And apparently your heartmate.... All I want to do is get back home."

"You have always been a Queen, Alice. Whether you knew it or not, your instincts are to protect people. To lead them. I see it in the way you carry yourself. Fearing your power will not give you control." He responded. "Let me help you. I will follow you to Earth, I'll learn their customs. My people are long gone, my oaths have been fulfilled."

"Okay." I breathed.

"Okay?" He seemed surprised, "You mean..."

"Take me inside, show me exactly who you really are."

Chapter 13

April 13th, 2159

My eyes fluttered open as fingers trailed down my belly, "Open for me, my Queen." Wyth's voice was husky from sleep, making it even sexier. I turned, spreading my legs wide. His fingers slid through my folds, causing me to buck my hips, "So responsive, so perfect. As if the Creator craved your body just for me." I moaned as his finger hooked inside of me, pressing against the exact spot that drove me over the edge. "Go ahead, my love, cum all over my fingers so I can take you." As if his words were enough, an orgasm zipped down my spine. Before it was over, Wyth had flipped me over, pulling my knees underneath me and sinking his cock deep into my pussy. He was thick, enough so that even though this was the third time we'd fucked my pussy still burned from the stretch of him. He was always gentle at first, ensuring that I was comfortable before he unleashed himself on me. I met him stroke for stroke, ignoring the pain of his powerful body snapping into my smaller one with such force the walls shook. My skin glowed, bright enough that I could see it through my closed eyelids, but when I opened them, I noticed Wyth's hand covering mine, glowing green overtop my silver.

I moved, and Wyth groaned, but allowed me to sit up. I pushed him backwards, forcing him to lay down before I sank back down on his cock again. I rode him slowly, running my hands over his naked chest, appreciating the differences in our bodies. In all the places I was soft, he was hard. I ran a finger over his nipple causing him to moan. "Why do we glow?"

His breath stuttered, but he managed to say, "Because our magick wants to be closer."

"But I glowed before we met, and not just once I met my husbands." I responded, before leaning down to run my tongue over his skin.

"Cruel vixen," He panted, "You are different from most magick users. Your magick is a living thing because you are a Queen. It cannot be contained like all other magick users."

"Hmmm. I guess that makes sense. Thank you." I bit down on his nipples, "Now why don't you cum for me so I can meet Duchess for our lesson."

He moaned as I quickened my pace, and within moments I felt his hot seed paint my inner walls. Once he had stopped shaking, I slowly climbed off of him, pressing a kiss to his cheek before I slipped into the bathroom to rinse off.

When I came back out, he was dressed and sitting on the end of the bed, "I think I'm going to join you today. Maybe I can assist Duchess on what a portal should be like since I've seen them before."

"We'll take any help we can get at this point." I shrugged, motioning for him to follow me.

As we made our way down the stairs, Dina came out of her room, "What are you doing?"

"Heading out for more magick lessons with Duchess. Wanna join?" I shouted back.

"Yes! I'm ready to go the fuck home. Why the fuck was Nova in my dark bathroom this morning?"

I laughcd, "She goes wherever she wants."

"You've spoiled that... thing already. Do you think she'll be okay when we leave?" Dina whispered as Nova climbed up my pant leg.

"She'll be going home with us." I responded, puzzled.

Dina stopped, "Alice, do you really think taking a creature from Undraland to Wonderland is a good idea? She won't have any of her own kind to socialize with."

I hadn't considered that. Nova had instantly become a part of me, but was taking her to Wonderland for the best? I ran my hand over her soft fur, "I promised Basha I would care for her. When Nova chose to be my companion, she chose to go with me where I go. When we go home, so will she."

Dina nodded, accepting my answer without any further argument. Wyth laid a hand on my shoulder, "I wonder how your husbands will feel about all the new followers you're bringing back to your home." I had no idea, but I couldn't let the anxiety of how they would react to Wyth cause me to drag my feet. I trusted my husbands to understand. We had been through so much together. My desire for Wyth didn't change my love for them. Dina needed to get back to Elsie, and I knew Wonderland needed me. He must have sensed my discomfort with the topic, because he leaned down and whispered, "From what you've told me, the love they have for you will trump any misgivings they may have."

"But I have been disloyal. I know that. Even if it can be explained by magick..." I muttered. Guilt did eat me alive at times, but I couldn't deny that being with the Emerald King felt... right. As if he'd been the missing piece in my heart.

"Is your relationship drama really the most important thing right now?" Duchess snapped as she stepped outside.

"No. Actually your magickal constipation is." I shot back. The stress of her portal magick was getting to all of us.

Dina snorted, but Wyth stepped in, "Let's just get started."

Hours passed and little to no progress was being made. Every time Duchess reached into my magick to power herself, there was another explosion of black dust.

"Stop reaching for Alice's magick. You were given the power to do this by the Creator. You don't need her to open a portal, the power lies inside of you." Wyth instructed as Dina and I took a seat watching from a few feet away, "Close your eyes. Reach down into your core, find the well of your magick." Several beats of silence passed as Duchess did what he instructed. Her hands suddenly glowed black, "Very good. Now imagine your home. Imagine the people you care for. Let your magick traverse to them." When a swirling black circle appeared before Duchess, Dina and I both jumped up. "Stay steady, you're doing great, Vivica. Now, imagine your magick as a doorway, allowing you and others to step through." The black swirl expanded, flickering images of our home flashed through. Dina rushed toward the portal. "No! Stop! You'll break her concentration." Wyth yelled, but Dina was already diving through the shimmering black portal. I noticed the sweat on Duchess' brow, the strain of her magick was visible.

I stepped to her side, laying a hand on her shoulder, "Just a few more minutes. Imagine my apartment, imagine the guys. We can step right to them." I muttered, watching as the portal shook and flickered. When it stopped, showing my living room with Hatter standing in the center I nearly squealed.

A muffled, "Alice?" floated through the portal to me. There were sounds of chaos from the other side, but the image was blurry.

"I can't hold it. Go through, Alice. Go. I'll get home eventually." Duchess' voice was hoarse.

I glanced at her, and back to Wyth, "No. I'm not leaving without you." Dina was already gone, and I prayed she had ended up back in Wonderland. "You can do this. Just step through with me."

Before we could move, the portal shook so hard the ground around us shook. I lost my footing, falling to my knees. Seconds before the world exploded in black dust, I saw four figures push through the rapidly closing portal.

Duchess passed out, Wyth managed to catch her before her head hit the ground, but that wasn't my biggest priority as I stood to my feet.

"Alice?" I turned at Caterpillar's voice, softer than I'd ever heard before. "Is that really you?"

Sobs burst from my throat as I took in the faces of the four men I loved most in the world. All of them were covered in soot, but they were alive. They were standing here in Undraland with me. I threw myself into the center of them. Hands and mouth colliding in a moment of pure desperation. I couldn't tell who was who as I was passed arm to arm, tears soaking through the shirts they wore.

"I've fucking missed you, princess. I'm seriously getting that leash. You're never to be out of my sight again." Caterpillar rumbled into my ear.

I laughed through my tears, "I think I might let you this time."

A small cough from behind us, reminded me that we weren't alone. Wyth had Duchess' unconscious body in his arms, "I'm sorry to interrupt your reunion, but I need to get her to Ledger for medical attention."

I rushed over to him without a second thought, laying my hand on Duchess' chest. I felt her magick, dormant and spent in her core, "She just needs to sleep."

Wyth nodded, "I'm still going to have Ledge give her one of his potions. It'll help her recover faster." He leaned and pressed a kiss to my forehead, "I'll leave you to the reunion for now."

When he disappeared back into the castle, I turned back to my husbands. Noting the varying looks of confusion and jealousy on their faces I sighed. "I was really hoping we could just enjoy that we're back together for a few minutes, before we... caught up."

Cheshire was the first one to speak, "Why did the very hot, very tall man kiss you?"

"No beating around the bush huh?" I joked, but the look on Caterpillar's face made me cringe, "Welcome to Undraland, Eumonia's home, and the original world of magick. Things are... different here."

Before I could continue, a bright flashing light filled the space between me and my husbands, *"Fear not children of Earth and Undraland. I am who you call the Creator."* I heard Hatter hiss, but I couldn't move or open my eyes, *"I apologize for my sudden appearance. I know your mortal eyes cannot look upon me, but I must speak with all of you now."*

"You're the Creator?" Caterpillar questioned, "Why have you abandoned Earth?"

An almost wistful sigh left the Creator, *"Hello, Roman Ainsworth. Your family was one of my most valiant in the old days. I see their warrior spirit in you. That is why I blessed you with my champion as your heartmate. Alice is my chosen, the only one who can fulfill Undraland's needs."* She sighed again, *"But I am getting ahead of myself. To answer your question, I am not the Creator of Earth, my sister is. I cannot control what she has done with her world. The powers that I have only reach to those that are blessed by my hand. The lines that fled Undraland with Eumonia."*

"I'm not feeling very blessed right now." Cheshire said, "My retinas may never recover."

A soft laugh left the Creator, and suddenly the light around her dimmed, *"Sinclair Malone, a descendant of the protector of the Shadelumes. I blessed your line with similar powers, but you have certainly held onto the good humor of your ancestors."*

March snorted, causing the Creator to say, "*And Maxton Danara. One of my favorite sons. I'm sorry that I could not help your pain but know that I am proud of how your power has evolved.*" March made a sound in his throat, but didn't respond to her praise, "*Alice Lyon has chosen her companions well. Even you, Hayden O'Hare. You are not a child of Undraland, but I heard your call when my champion was harmed, and I have blessed you with a piece of my power.*"

Suddenly, his white hair and strange magick clicked into place. After months, I finally understood why healing drained him. He wasn't born a magick user. The Creator had used him to save my life. "As her Knights, I have blessed your bonds and created a lifelong connection between you. You are her heartmates. A bond that cannot be broken by gods or mortals. But I have blessed her with another, my Emerald King. Wyth of Undraland will be her Knight as well. Together the six of you will save our world, and rule over Undraland. Queen Alice Lyon and Her Silver Kings."

"Do we not get a say in who she is with?" March asked, surprising me, "Does she?"

"*A heartmate cannot be denied. Would you ask her to leave one of you?*" The Creator's voice was stern now, nearly authoritative. Her patience was running out, "*She is my champion, her task requires more power than any Queen before her has had. It is your job as her heartmates to ensure that she is protected.*"

"We will do our duty." Caterpillar said, "Thank you for blessing us with our wife."

A flood of warmth ran through my body, and seconds later the light faded away, leaving us all blinking and confused. "So that was the Creator?" Cheshire said, "Not as... masculine as I would have expected."

Caterpillar smacked the back of his head, "Shut the fuck up. That was literally our Creator."

"Well yours anyway. It sounds like my Creator kind of sucks." Hatter added, before turning to me, "Sweetheart, it's so good to see you."

Tears welled in my eyes again, "I've missed you all so much."

"Apparently not too much. With your new h-heartmate." March snapped.

"March." Hatter chastised, "I know none of us are excited about the prospect of sharing Alice with someone else, but it wasn't her choice. They were bound together by forces more powerful than us."

March rolled his eyes, "Maybe s-so, but clearly they had no trouble getting started while we were all worried she was dead."

I held up my hands in defeat, "I know why you're upset, and it's valid to feel betrayed. I just hope you can understand... Wyth and I care for one another. I was never looking to replace any of you. I love you all differently, but equally. My feelings for him change *nothing* about my feelings for you."

March didn't respond, but Cheshire said, "Who gives a fuck about that guy right now. Let's go consummate our marriage."

Caterpillar snorted, but the fire in his eyes told me all I needed to know, "Follow me." I said as I lead them through the garden and into the castle.

Hatter gawked at the double doors that led inside, "What are these made out of? Looks like marble, but it feels like wood."

"Things here are... similar but different. Eventually, you just get used to it." I explained as we continued to walk to my room.

"I have so many questions," Cheshire said as we entered my bedroom, "But none of them matter. Strip and get on the bed."

I didn't have to be told twice. I was so ready to rejoin with my husbands. The men I loved were here. Of course, that was its own problem. Wonderland was undefended, and it was possible Duchess would never be able to get us home. But right now, the only thing that mattered was that I needed to be with the men I loved.

Caterpillar was naked before my face first, his long, thick cock bobbing in my vision, "Take me in your mouth, princess." I swallowed him instantly, my nose pressing against the base of him. He groaned, fingers wrapping into my hair, "My perfect wife." He muttered, as he fucked my throat relentlessly.

Hands trailed over my body, too many of them to know who they belonged to, but when a cock pressed against my ass I had no doubt it was Cheshire. I pushed back, fighting the pain of my muscles stretching. I needed them too much to care about a little pain.

Caterpillar pulled away, allowing Hatter to lift and move me until he was under me, sliding into my dripping pussy. Once they were both comfortable, Caterpillar returned to my mouth, viciously slamming into my throat, until he slipped his cum over my tongue.

Cheshire and Hatter kept a steady rhythm, pushing and pulling out in tandem so that I could never catch my breath. Caterpillar's lips slammed down on mine, his fingers reaching down to tweak my nipples, "I love seeing you so full of cock you can't even think."

I moaned, as March came into view, his cock weeping precum. "Please Maxton, let me help you."

He sighed, "I can't resist you, Ali." He climbed onto the bed, allowing me to suck him into my mouth. He was gentle at first, allowing me to set the pace, but when Hatter groaned, his cock pulsing into my pussy, he grabbed my chin, forcing me to take him deeper. My jaw ached as he fucked my face without remorse. When Cheshire gripped my hips, groaning as he came in my ass March slammed his cock down my throat, cumming in tandem.

I was panting as he pulled away, but Caterpillar was there, lifting me and turning me over, "So full of your husbands' cum. Do you feel good, princess?"

I nodded, unable to find my words. His hands ran over my body, careful of the sensitive areas, "Would you like to cum for us?" I moaned in response, spreading my legs, "Touch yourself. Show us how much you loved us taking you."

I followed his instructions, rubbing my clit in fast circles, moaning as they all began to touch me. Hands pulled on my nipples, as Hatter sunk his fingers into my pussy. When Caterpillar's hand wrapped around my throat I fell over the edge, my orgasm causing me to black out.

When I came back to I was redressed and tucked under my blankets. The men surrounded me on all sides, "Welcome back sweetheart."

"I've missed you all so much." I blurted out, before pulling Hatter in for a kiss.

"We've missed you too. We're nothing without you." Cheshire said, before kissing me.

"I don't know what's going to happen next, but I'm glad we'll be together." Caterpillar said, pressing a kiss to my forehead.

March and I stared at each other for a long time, "I love you, Ali, b-but I'm hurt right now."

I nodded, holding his hand, "It's going to take time to adjust." March pressed a kiss to my cheek, before pulling away to cuddle with Hatter.

Slowly I settled down, allowing the warmth of my husbands to lull me to sleep. Now that we were together again, I had no doubt we would find a way to get back home and do whatever the Creator had planned for me.

Chapter 14

April 15th, 2159

Duchess was still recovering; her magick had drained completely. Edik was insisting that she stay in bed and take a break from training for at least five days. In the meantime, I'd taken to showing the guys around the castle and its grounds. Wyth had been notably absent since they'd arrived, and I was starting to get annoyed with his avoidance.

I stomped through the eastern wing of the castle, finally stopping at Wyth's door. Before I could knock, it swung open. Wyth stood in nothing but a towel, water droplets running down every inch of his skin, "Good morning, my Queen. What can I do for you?"

"Drop your bullshit, Wyth. Why are you acting differently?" I snapped.

Wyth reached out, wrapping a hand around my bicep and yanking me into the room before slamming the door shut, "My Knights are also housed on this floor, and I'd prefer they didn't hear our lovers' quarrels." Wyth gritted out, "Your husbands are here now. I was giving you space to spend time with them."

"Everyone wants to get to know you," That was mostly the truth. March was still on the fence, but he was working on it, "How can they do that if you're avoiding me?"

He sighed, "Alice... You mean a lot to me. I don't want to get in the way of your happiness."

"You're getting in your own fucking way. Come have lunch with us, and I thought I might take the guys for a walk to show them around Undraland more after."

"Give me time to get dressed." He ordered me out of the room with that, but I still took it as a win. I already cared for Wyth, I wanted him to fit in with the guys so that... I couldn't let my mind go further. Nothing would be right until we returned to Wonderland.

Lunch was a small and slightly awkward affair. Hatter and Cheshire did their best to chat with Wyth. Caterpillar was his usual brooding self, hovering as close to me as possible, a watchful eye on my newest addition. It felt odd to admit to myself that Wyth was a permanent fixture in my life. I barely knew him. Even less than I'd known the guys when we'd started dating if I was being honest with myself. Yet there was something about him, something that fit with me, made me feel safe and secure... I knew I'd love him just as much as I loved each of my husbands one day. Sooner than anyone would believe.

Now I watched as March and Hatter walked ahead of us on the path Wyth had brought us to. Apparently, some of my ancestors had been avid hikers, cutting paths throughout Undraland to explore and witness the creatures they had been charged with caring for. I glanced toward Cheshire who strolled on my left. He sauntered with a confidence that made me so attracted to him I could jump him right there. He was growing, different than he had been when we first met. "I still don't like hiking, Al. You'll never convince me that its fun."

Wyth snorted, "It isn't. I've marched with my Knights for days. It's may be necessary, but it certainly isn't fun."

"He just gets better and better." Cheshire said, "A man after my heart."

"I'm sorry, I only desire Alice's heart. I'd accept your kinship or brotherhood though." Wyth responded seriously.

Cheshire and I stopped walking, glancing at each other before we both burst into laughter. Caterpillar and Wyth both turned back and stood mimicking one another with their arms crossed as they watched Cheshire and I fall into fits of laughter. When we saw them, both looking so serious and confused we laughed harder.

"What is wrong with them?" Wyth asked.

"I've been asking myself that since I met them." Caterpillar responded, "It's not worth puzzling over too much. You'll never understand it."

I snorted, "Oh, Cater baby, I've missed you so much. I'm so glad you have a father to your mother hen now."

Cheshire howled, "God I'm so glad I married you, woman."

Caterpillar shook his head, but I could see the small smirk on his face, "Let's keep moving we've lost Hatter and March."

When we caught up to them, they were on their knees in front of a large stump.

"Be quiet," Hatter snapped, as we came fully into sight. "Look what we found." March turned, revealing two small creatures curled in his arms. I moved closer, at first mistaking one for a Shadelume due to its fluffy pale green fur. Instead, I noticed feathered white wings resting against its haunches. When I took in its face, I realized is sort of resembled the drawings of rabbits I'd seen on earth. Though its eye were rounder, the tiny fangs jutted from its mouth, along with small horns, it could easily be mistaken for a pet bunny. Once I'd admired the white one for several moments, my eyes drifted to its siblings. Fur as black as night that seemed to absorb the light. Its wings weren't feathered, instead the skin ended in sharp points.

"What are they?" I turned so Wyth could see what March held.

"Burrowyn." He responded, "Generally these guys are pretty tame, so long as you don't startle them."

"What happens-" Cheshire wasn't able to finish his sentence, because Hatter howled. We all turned back to find they tiny green Burrowyn attached to Hatter's hand. He held his arm aloft, the Burrowyn hanging by its teeth from his palm. Blood already leaked from the wounds.

"Creator above." Wyth cried, pushing past me to gently grip the Burrowyn. Green magic surrounded his hands, and the creature relaxed, releasing Hatter from its grip. As soon as he was free, Hatter pitched forward his skin paling. "Take her. You need to bring them with us in case Ledger needs them for an anti-venom. They seem to like you so try to keep everyone else from touching them." He spoke directly to March, before turning to Caterpillar, "I'll need help carrying him back." Together the two of them got Hatter up between them, each of them taking one of his arms over their necks. "We have to move quickly. We're not far from the castle."

"What's happening?" I asked as we nearly ran back over the path. March trailed behind jogging more than walking to avoid upsetting the Burrowyn's he'd now been tasked with caring for.

"Burrowyn's have a venomous bite. We have to get Hatter to Ledger for an antidote, or the bite could be fatal." Wyth explained, his voice far too calm for the situation at hand.

Cheshire ran past me, "I'll go ahead, find your Knight so he's prepared." Wyth nodded at him, and within seconds Cheshire had disappeared, faster than I'd ever seen anyone move before.

When Wyth noticed my face he said, "Undraland won't just enhance your powers. It will enhance theirs as well."

I hadn't considered that. The longer we ran the more my mind raced over the possibility of Undraland changing us all. Seeping into our bones and changing us on a molecular level. In some ways, I could already feel the ways those changes had affected me. I was stronger, more settled in my magic than ever. My thoughts were clearer too, less fogged by emotion. Maybe we were changing for the better, becoming who we were always meant to be.

When we finally arrived at the castle, Cheshire and Ledger were already waiting. Ledger barked orders as soon as he appeared, "Take them into my room, I've set up small cage with wooden shavings to keep them happy temporarily." He produced a small green vial from his pocket, "Tilt his head back, we need to give them this potion now."

"What is it?" March asked, ignoring the instructions he'd been given.

Ledger didn't stop moving, gripping either side of Hatter's face and dumping the vial known his throat, "It's my last Knights Healing Potion. You'd better pray to the Creator it works."

March looked stricken before he quickly rushed to take the Burrowyns to Ledger's room. The world slowed at those words, and I closed my eyes. Reaching with my senses and my magick, "*I know you can hear me. Please, help the potion work. Don't make me lose him when we just reunited. I'll do anything for you. Just please save him.*"

Several silent beats passed, and I feared I would not get a response. That my desperate prayer would not be heard. Eventually a small voice whispered in my ear, "*Your heartmate is safe. The magick I left inside of him will work with the potion to keep him alive.*"

"*Thank you.*"

I didn't get a response, but I didn't expect one. The Creator was an all-powerful being, who had already saved the man I loved multiple times. Wyth settled Hatter on the center of my bed. His coloring was better, but the white in the front of his hair had spread more, as if the color had been sapped from it. It was more obvious than it had been before. As his breathing evened out, I felt the tension melt from my shoulders.

March reappeared, running his long fingers over Hatter's jawline, "I'm s-sorry. I shouldn't have insisted on t-touching them."

"Don't blame yourself. The creatures of Undraland are far more unpredictable than they were in the old days. I've never seen a Burrowyn attack anyone unprovoked like that." Wyth chimed in.

March looked at him for a moment, but giving a quiet, "Thank you."

Once Hatter returned to his normal coloring and breathing pattern everyone slowly left the room, leaving me alone with March as we watched our husband's peaceful sleeping face.

"He's going to be okay." I reassured him, "And Wyth's right. It isn't your fault."

"He's a nice man." March said, turning to face me, "I can already see the camaraderie between him and C-Caterpillar."

"That doesn't change that me being with him scares you." I pointed out softly.

March snorted, "You've always read me so well. I'll never be able to hide anything from you."

"I don't want you to. I want you to be who you are. The wonderful man I married. If that means that it takes you time to accept Wyth, then so be it." I said.

"If he loves you, I'll learn to like him." March responded, seriously. "He saved Hatter's life today. I can't ignore that."

"Glad me almost dying is all it takes for you to be buddy buddy with Alice's new boy toy." Hatter groaned from his spot on the bed.

I laughed as tears welled in my eyes. March threw himself against Hatter's chest, "I'm so glad you're alive."

"You two aren't rid of my yet." He responded, gripping my hand, "I told you a long time ago. As long as we're together, everything will be okay."

Hatter was right. I'd heard it many times, but it meant more now that we'd been separated by an entire world. We'd found each other again, and I'd never stop fighting for them. Even if I had to cross time and space to get to them, I would love Hatter, March, Caterpillar, and Cheshire until I was dust in the wind. Soon enough the Emerald King would be included in that list as well.

Chapter 15

Wyth

April 20th, 2159

I crept along the edge of the woods, watching as the Bandersnatch crashed through the forest blindly. In the back of my mind, I knew I'd seen this before. Had lived the next moments of my life hundreds of times, but it was always a thrill when the giant white beast rushed me. I caught it around the waist, slamming it into the ground, as I raised the Vorporal sword to slice off its head. I hesitated. Something was different this time though... This time I stared into the dark depths of its eyes, the world around me pausing. I glanced up, squinting my eyes as the shining figure of a woman standing several feet down the path.

I straightened, abandoning the death blow I'd been about to deal. As soon as I focused on the figure the creature vanished, as if it had never existed.

I walked toward the warm light that now pulsed brighter, kneeling in lieu of a greeting.

"Stand, my son." The Creator's voice echoed in his ears, layered in a way that made its true gender impossible to tell. "I'm sorry to interrupt your reminiscing."

I snorted, "Reminiscing on death in the presence of the being that created my world feels... inappropriate."

A soft laugh tinkled in his ears, "You should be proud of your accomplishments."

"I've never found pride in killing, only in protecting my people." I couldn't stop the words as they fell off my tongue.

"That is why I came, Wythandian. You only care for protecting those that you love. It is why I have bound you to the young Lyon Queen. She shares this quality with you, but I fear she will crumble if she does not learn that losing people she loves is a cost everyone pays." They explained, "There are stirrings across the worlds. The final battle draws nearer. Train, only you have the powers to bring them all to their full potential."

"I will do what I can, but Alice is strong. She won't stop fighting." I responded. "Am I meant to reveal all of my power to my heartmate and her harem?"

"Do what your heart leads you to do, my son. It is your greatest power of all."

I awoke with a new purpose, but I did not go to Alice's side. I knew she was still fawning over Hatter, who was soaking up the attention, even if he had been better for several days now. I liked Alice's husbands, could see the kinship growing between us, but I had been a solitary leader all of my life. Until I was certain of how they would react, I had to follow my next steps alone.

My first stop was with Edik. He lounged in his room; his helmet sat on his nightstand. His blonde hair was cropped short, something I'd never seen on him before, but the stubble along his jaw was even more shocking.

"It's not often I see you resting, Ed." Edik jumped up, reaching for his helmet on instinct, "Stop. Stop. It's fine, Ed. Just here as a friend, not your leader."

"You startled me," He said, "What can I do for you?"

"You seem to have some fondness for Duchess. I'm wondering if you'd be willing to join me while I talk to her." Edik's face molted red, but I filed the information away for later, "It's imperative that she learns how to harness her magick."

"You can't force her to accept it." He responded with a sigh, "She's stubborn. The harder she's pushed, the more she's going to dig her heels in and continue to avoid it."

"She nearly succeeded though. If we can convince her to get past her block, she will be a huge asset in Undraland." I explained.

"Don't say that for sure. She's... From what I've gathered, magick is a sore spot for her due to experiences from her childhood." Edik rubbed the back of his neck, "Has Alice given you any more information on what exactly has been going on since Earth and Undraland became disconnected?"

She had actually. Late one night, after he'd spent hours tasting her, she'd explained what she knew about Eumonia and the city she had saved on Earth. He had no problem believing his old friend had done such powerful feats of magick; he just didn't understand why Rhosyn had betrayed her entire world. How had she gained immortality, a gift reserved for the strongest magick users? None of it made any sense to him. He'd known these women, had spent hours with them, planning out how to care for their world as it devolved into illness and chaos. All the while, Rhosyn had been plotting against them as a child of the Red King... It was too much to wrap his brain around. "None of it is good." I responded.

"What can we do to help the Queen and Duchess?" Edik asked. He had always been a pillar of duty and responsibility. I couldn't be happier to have him by my side in this situation.

"Somehow, we need to help Duchess with her magick. It's the only way for them to return to Earth." I said.

"What are we going to do when they leave? The Creator tasked the Queen with saving Undraland. How is she going to do that from another world?" He brought up great questions... Unfortunately, I didn't have the answers.

"I'm going to go with Alice... I have to. She's my heartmate." I had to be honest with my Knights. It was part of our code. "You have to decide for yourself if you're going to stay here and protect Undraland or follow us."

Edik nodded, "I'll talk to Duchess. Just give me some time. I think I can get through to her."

"Thank you, brother." I clasped my hand on his shoulder, leaning my head against his in respect.

Before I could leave the room, he said, "Wyth... You should take the time to get to know Alice's other heartmates. They seem like good men."

I didn't answer him, but I knew he was right. I'd held myself apart from them, insecure that I would never fit in with them. The comradery and bond between all four of them was undeniable. They had been brothers-in-arms before they fell in love with Alice, and she'd only brought them closer together. I didn't want to insert myself where I was not wanted, but I loved Alice. I had to try. I left Edik with my mission, sending a prayer to the Creator that he could get through to Duchess. I had other things to attend to.

I found Caterpillar walking the grounds, his eyes scanned his surroundings as he wandered around the outside of the maze. Occasionally stopping, squatting down to test the hedge. It shook, shrinking away from his touch. I'd already felt the strange, blankess of his magick. It had taken me time to place that it was a void power, but I'd recognized his last name immediately. The Ainsworth's were the Phoenix's of old. Essentially immortal if their funeral rite was completed correctly. It was a major asset, and I had no doubt he'd use it to protect Alice any chance he could.

When he noticed me, he straightened, "Is Alice okay?"

"I believe she's with Hatter." I answered. "I actually came to talk to you."

His eyebrow arched at my words, but he said, "What can I do for you?" My words dried up. I realized for the first time in my life, I wasn't sure how to handle this situation. I'd tried to be respectful, if distant, and that had only upset my heartmate. Now I stood before the clear leader of her husbands, and I had no idea what to say. He must have realized that I had frozen, because he said, "You know Cheshire seems to really like you, and Hatter's warming up. March is a complicated man, so I wouldn't take any of his dislike to heart."

"And what about you? How do you feel about me?" I asked.

"Walk with me." He waved, turning back to the hedge. Once again, swooping down and reaching toward it. I squatted next to him, watching as the vines shrilved away from his hand as if it was poison. When he stood back up, moving forward as if nothing happened, he said, "I didn't know I had any magick until Alice was kidnapped by a man named Dnais. He stabbed me, and when Hatter and Alice's mother tried to heal me it didn't work. I died..." He trailed off for a long moment, continuing our walk in silence, "I've never told Alice or the guys... But I remember snippets of it... My afterlife. It was peaceful, but there was something missing. When I started to come back to my body, I was excited. Alice had been the only thing I could think about. I think the Creator spoke to me during that time, but... It's too fuzzy. Too far away. I'm grateful for my Uncle, who had held onto the traditions of my family, without him I'd never be able to return."

"It must have been a shock to come back." I said, watching his profile.

"I haven't thought about it, because the only thing that truly mattered to me even in death is my wife." He turned to face me, his grey eyes swirling with a storm of emotion, "So long as she wants you I'll accept you as my brother. The others are younger, but their love for her is no different than mine... Just know, if you ever hurt her, I don't give a fuck what the Creator says. I'll end your life."

I grinned, "That's all I expect of you." Weight lifted from my shoulders as he reached out his hand. I took it, clasping his wrist as I would my Knights, "To loving our woman and protecting our worlds."

"To loving our woman and protecting our worlds." He echoed.

Chapter 16

Alice

April 22nd, 2159

I'd found some kind of normal routine since the guys had stepped into Undraland. I spent my mornings with them, before exploring the castle. Sometimes alone, sometimes someone would join me. Today, I found myself on the top floor, what should have been an attic was instead an inside garden. The roof was glass, allowing the suns to light the room. The plants were mostly unfamiliar, so I stayed away from them, occasionally sniffing a flower seemed safe enough. I found a small sitting area with plush couches and found myself lounging, basking in the sun. I was coming to love the castle, every new discovery made me feel closer to a family I would never have the chance to know. I ached to show my mother all the details of the castle, she would love it. I imagined a world where things were different. Where Eumonia had never gone to Earth. Would I have grown up in these walls? I shook my head. My father was from Earth, it had been my home my entire life. I wouldn't let myself abandon it so easily, not when my mother and sister were still in Wonderland. Fighting the Queen of Hearts alone. Guilt flooded me, I'd become too complacent since my husbands had come to Undraland. I'd been imagining a life here, as if I could forget the rest of my family.

I stood, knowing I needed to try to talk to Duchess, but before I could take a single step Wyth appeared a panicked look on his face, "I need you to come downstairs now."

I didn't ask questions, rushing after him as he turned to run. As soon as we hit the base of the stairs, I gasped. Sporekin was sitting against the wall, his chest was torn open, a greenish fluid leaking from some pf the wounds. The baby Sporekin's had grown significantly since I'd last seen them. Now reaching to my hip. All ten of them were curled around their father, concern and fear clear on their faces.

"What happened?" I asked, kneeling before the giant creature.

"The tree... was attacked..." Every word was seemingly painful. "I tried to save it, Queen Alice." Sporekin cried out as he began to cough.

Caterpillar appeared, followed by Cheshire.

"That's a talking mushroom." Cheshire said, "Talking cats, talking mushrooms... what's next? Talking flowers."

Wyth couldn't help himself, "The Dandifolds were the first race to go extinct when the illness came."

"Go get, Hatter." I commanded, "Sporekin needs to be healed." Caterpillar opened his mouth to argue, but something on my face stopped him. "Just take it easy. We're going to take care of you." I ignored the tears that began to prick the back of my eyes. I was very fond of Sporekin, I didn't want him to die. One of the babies seemed to sense my emotions, curling into my lap. I ran a hand over its head, "What's your name, little one?"

It opened its mouth, emitting sounds I couldn't understand. Sporekin translated, "Sorry, Queen... They're too young... to easily absorb your language... No names... We are Sporekin."

Before I could respond, Caterpillar returned with Hatter and March in tow. Hatter kneeled next to me, resting one of his hands on my thigh as the white glow of his healing magick wrapped around his other hand. I felt his magick reach for mine, and I opened myself up to it without hesitation. Hatter laid his hand against Sporekin's chest, and we all waited with bated breath as the magick seeped into his thick, dark sienna skin. The wounds knit together before our eyes, Sporekin's breathing slowly returned to normal. His wide brown eyes fluttered closed.

"Let's find him and the babies a room." I said, standing, "He'll need to rest before we figure out what happened."

"I'll send Kori and Ledger to investigate the tree." Wyth said, "Edik is busy working with Duchess."

I raised an eyebrow at that information, but didn't have time to ask questions as the guys all moved to lift Sporekin. It took all five of my men to carry him to a room, depositing him on the bed as the babies made noise in their language. They swarmed around my legs, occasionally hugging. I bent down, unsure the best way to communicate with them. March kneeled next to me, "Th-they're very cute."

"My magick helped create them." I ran my hand over one of their heads, "I want to name them. I know Sporekin said no, but it would help if I could tell them apart."

March jumped up, rushing from the room without a word. When he returned he had his arms full of varying colors of ribbon. "I can make them little bracelets. Th-that way you can tell them apart without disrespecting his request."

"Where did you find all of this?" I asked as I sorted through the ribbon. I picked out a sunny yellow color, showing it to the baby Sporekin in my lap, "Can I put this on you?" It stared at me quizzically, glancing down at the ribbon. When it finally gave a small nod, I cut a long piece, tying it around its thick wrist. The baby cooed in its strange language, nuzzling against my hand before turning to show its siblings the ribbon.

"There's a room with all sorts of things like this. I even found some yarn." March answered as he presented a blue ribbon to one of the babies. "I swear it's l-like the castle knows what we love, and ensures its available to us."

I considered that as we continued to tie colorful ribbons around the Sporekin's wrists. Every time I was wandering the halls, I came across something that made me feel more at ease... more at home. The entirety of Undraland was magick. Why hadn't it crossed my mind that the castle was as well? Alive in its own way. Welcoming its royalty with open arms. Once the Sporekin babies were all settled down around their father, March and I left the room. "Will you show me the room you found?" When we'd first arrived at the castle, many of the rooms had been covered in dust. The Knights, Dina, and I had worked to clean the primary areas for us, but as I thought about what March said, I'd realized each new room I found was in perfect condition.

We walked hand in hand down to the room he'd mentioned. As we entered any doubt I'd had about the magick of the castle disappeared. The room was painted in a soft green, three of the four walls had shelves full of different fabric and crafting materials. All of it looked new. "What a welcome." I muttered as I explored the space. It was exactly the room I would have created for March, quiet, sunny, and full of his favorite hobby. "I feel manipulated."

"Why?" March asked as he picked up a project he'd clearly started recently. A baby blue yarn with an otherworldly sparkle to it.

I didn't speak for a long moment, watching as he began to crochet with a speed I couldn't imagine. "The Creator has literally tasked me with saving this world... Until you guys got here I spent my time focused on returning to Wonderland. But now?" I sighed, throwing myself on the couch next to him, "I feel like everyone expects me to just stay here. To be the Queen, and forget about my family on Earth. I'm not willing to do that."

"Is th-that what Wyth wants you to do?" There was an edge to the question.

I sighed, "I thought you were warming up to him..."

March dropped his project, turning to face me, "J-just because he helped save Hatter's life doesn't mean I'm just going to accept him. I see the way you're struggling t-to figure out what to do. He isn't helping with that at all. He's making it worse. Making you feel like you have to be Queen of Undraland instead of returning to your h-home."

I stood, pacing, "What if I want to be the Queen of Undraland? What if I do love it here?" I turned toward him, "It's not Wyth's fault that I feel this way. Blaming him isn't fair. I understand that I hurt you by falling for him before I got back to you, but... It happened, March. You're not actually mad at him. You're mad at me."

"B-but I can't be mad at you." He snapped, "I don't want to be mad at you. You're my wife. I love you..."

"But?" I pushed him, knowing we needed to deal with these feelings.

"You're going to abandon me for this place. For all the things the Emerald King, Undraland, and the Creator have to offer you. And I can't even b-blame you. I love it here too!"

The breath rushed out of me. "I'd never leave you, March. I swear it."

A tear rolled down his cheek, "Just when I'd finally started to heal. I met my father, Alice... I stood up for myself with my mother. Now I may never see him again... and you're going to replace me."

"I could never replace you, Maxton." I pulled him into a hug, "And I promise you, we are going to back to Wonderland. I don't know what I've learned here truly means, but I owe it to our family and to the citizens of Wonderland."

We embraced, March's lips crashing into mine with a fervor I wasn't prepared for. I moaned as his fingers tangled into my hair, pulling my head back gently so he had more access. He pulled away panting, "I've f-fucking missed you, Ali."

"I've missed you too." I muttered, leaning my forehead against his, "No matter what happens, I will love you until both worlds are barren and the Creators have died."

Even within the castle, night felt different in Undraland. More sinister. I couldn't sleep, between the attack on Sporekin and my realizations about the magick of the castle my mind was racing. So I found myself roaming the halls, the glow of my magick casting eerie shadows along the walls. I made my way down into the basement, back to the golden well where the Creator had first spoken to me. I stared into its black depths, expecting to find answers to my unspoken questions. Instead, I found only silence. The Creator wasn't going to guide my every move, she never had been. She'd only gifted me boons on occasion. I wanted to lean on my husbands, but I could see the uncertainty in all of their eyes. They didn't know how to get home, what to do for Undraland, why the Queen of Hearts had truly done when she'd stranded me here. I felt like there was some purpose, some deeper plan, but I was blind to her machinations. I always had been.

I sighed, standing to stretch my aching legs. A sound of doors closing drew my attention, so I headed up the stairs. I didn't get far before I saw Kori limping toward his bedroom. I rushed to his side, "Are you okay?"

"Yes, Alice. Ledger and I got caught by Noxroots as we were returning to the castle, they've been roaming closer and closer. We handled them, there's no need for you to be worried." I could tell from the strain in his voice, he was hurt.

"Do you need healing? I can wake Hatter up." I offered.

He shook his head, his helmet causing a metal noise to echo through the halls, "I'm fine, my Queen. You should return to your rest."

"What did you find at the tree?" I asked, before he could turn away. He froze, tensing at my question.

"Ledger is preparing a report for the King in the morning. I think it would be best if you both heard it together." His words were stiff, almost rehearsed.

"I'm sure Wyth would understand, he's asleep right now. I'm not. Tell me what you found." I insisted.

"I really should lay down, so my natural healing can kick in. Did you know that all Undralandian's have increased healing abilities?"

I snorted, "Kori, come on. I'm not stupid. What's going on?"

He sighed, "You better butter Wyth up, so he doesn't kill me for telling you before him."

"I'll handle him." I waved him off.

"I'm sure you will," He muttered, "There was evidence of the Jabberwock. It looked as if the tree had been scorched by its lightning breath. The inside was ransacked, as if someone had gone through the tree looking for something. Whatever harmed Sporekin wasn't the only being there."

"The Jabberwock?" Jabberwocky cutting into me flashed through my brain, my scars tightening at the memory. My heart raced in my chest, but I forced myself to say, "Sorry, Kori. I still don't know all of Undraland's creatures."

"The Jabberwock is a legendary beast, no one alive had ever seen it in person. Just rumors that it roamed the mountains to the East, seeking to destroy the Tumtum tree. It looks like it finally found it." Kori shuttered, "It's worse than the Bandersnatch. Wyth will want to hunt it down, kill it before it can harm anything else."

"Thanks for explaining. Go rest, you earned it." Kori inclined his head, and continued his trek to his room. Once he was out of sight, I turned running to the library. Something itched in my brain, and I knocked down a pile of books I'd been reading through, hunting until I came across the correct book. I flipped through it, finding the grainy image. It was the same tree Sporekin had brought us to when we'd first landed in Undraland.

Underneath the picture, bold black letter declared it the Tumtum tree, a mythical place where the Creator originally created the world. Sacred to the Lyon Queens, because the crown of the next Queen appeared there before their coronation. My stomach rolled, the silver tiara of twisted vines that currently sat in my nightstand. One of the first things I'd touched after entering Undraland. The moment I'd placed it on my head, I'd accepted my role as Queen of this world. I hadn't even known. Now, it had been attacked, nearly destroyed if I'd understood what Kori had been implying. My magick buzzed under my skin as I stormed back downstairs, to the well, rage turned to electricity snapping along my skin.

"She's here, isn't she?" I shouted into the dark, cavernous space. "The Queen of Hearts, destroyed that tree, hunting for that crown. For me now." My voice bounced off the walls, but I received no answer. Only my gut twisting into knots let me know my instincts were right. In a single moment, the bubble of peace of the castle had been popped. It was time to return to Wonderland and end the Queen of Heart's reign of terror for good. I didn't care what I had to sacrifice, I couldn't let anyone else be hurt by her.

Chapter 17

Eumonia

April 24ᵗʰ, 2159

"The people are riotous. We have to tell them the truth." Alcinda's words were grave, but her golden told me just how concerned she was. All of the leaders of Wonderland were now gone. When we'd found Caterpillar, Cheshire, Hatter, and March missing I'd known we were in trouble. Dina's story of Undraland gave me no hope. She didn't know what had happened with the portal. For all we knew, Alice was trapped between worlds. Meanwhile, Wonderland's citizens were demanding an appearance. I'd done by best to ease their fears, but Alice was not as well-known and respected as Caterpillar. The magick users were the only reasons everyone else hadn't already rioted. Their trust in Alice for saving them from the Red Queen, meant we had a group of people on our side. It wasn't enough anymore.

"Give me one more day. Let me see if I can find her, if I can end this myself." I begged, meeting the exhausted eyes of everyone in the room. I knew I couldn't. I wished a vision would give me some guidance, but I hadn't had a single one in weeks. I waited with bated breath each night, waiting for something... anything... But I'd been left waiting. Now, I had to take action.

"Do you think you can?" White Rabbit asked, "You've spent over a century choosing inaction."

His words stung, but it was true. The moment I'd wiped my memory from my daughter's mind I'd been choosing to wait. To witness. Now my legacy was scattered across the worlds as Wonderland's stirrings became violent. Whatever Rhosyn was doing was working. "I don't know, but we can't sit here and do nothing. Telling the citizens we've been lying to them for months, doesn't seem better." I sighed, "Figure out a story they might be able to swallow. Azura and I are going to hunt for her. If I don't return by tomorrow morning, tell Wonderland the truth. Fear may be all we have left."

I stood, leaving the room. Azura was already waiting for me as I stepped out into the rain. The weather in Wonderland had been dismal, and I had no doubt it was part of Rhosyn's plan. Spring should have begun, flowers blooming, and allowing people a distraction from the tension in the air. I pulled the hood of my coat lower over my face and walked with purpose. I'd never figured out the cars and bikes my grandchildren used, even when I'd first settled in Wonderland, I'd stayed far away from the motorized vehicles. Walking gave me more information; I could witness my city for myself. I headed toward the sixth district, magick leading me there. I'd noticed the pull two days before, something familiar, but... painful emanating from my former home. I splashed through deep puddles, carefully avoiding eye contact with any of the humans that passed me by. But I still heard their whispers, discontent and fearful. Attacks had grown bolder in the recent weeks, buildings burned to the ground in minutes, people vanishing from the streets. It was headed toward a fever pitch.

I slipped into my old home with ease, scanning the room, as I ran my fingers over the murals I'd painted of Undraland when I'd first moved in. They were fading now, but I still found solace in the images. As I made my way through the room, I searched for anything out of place. As I turned to glance at my bed, my breath stopped, my heart stuttering.

On my pillow, a golden crown with diamonds and onyx gems rested innocently. But the feelings that arose as I picked it up were a storm. It was my mother's. The crown I'd laid to rest in the Tumtum tree when I'd taken the throne as a child. The Sporekin, though small in number, had been protectors of the tree for thousands of years. They would never have allowed anyone to step into the sacred tree and take the crown. No... Rhosyn had somehow stolen this crown. To mock me. To show her power, and most of all... To let me know that she could still reach Undraland.

I dropped to my knees, clutching the crown that had once belonged to my mother. I couldn't stop the tears that rolled down my face. My best friend, a woman I had believed dead for over a hundred years, had betrayed me. Had locked me away from my kingdom and my people. Stranded me on Earth and ensured I could never return home. It hit me all at once, every memory shifting to live in this new context. I reached for anger but found none. Just bone-deep sorrow and fear for my family filled me.

"I have to do something, Azura. I have to try to help Alice." I muttered, reaching for the hidden box under my bed. I opened it, staring at the crown I had not worn in nearly a hundred and fifty years. It was covered in dust, its usually shining golden hue dimmed. The pale blue stones caught what light existed in the room, and I saw my reflection. I looked the same way I had at thirty-two when I stepped onto Earth. Rhosyn hadn't aged either. But so much had changed. I was not the same Queen I had been, I wasn't a Queen at all now. I was the matriarch of the Lyon women, and I would do anything to save Alcinda, Lily, and Alice. They were my true legacy.

Azura chirped, letting me know we were close to our destination. I cut through another vine that snaked toward me. Earth wasn't inhabitable outside of Wonderland. I don't know how Rhosyn survived with the plant and animal life constantly attacking any living thing it could. The tower we approached was crumbling, clearly a relic of the old world that had long been destroyed. But I could see smoke drifting from its half-destroyed chimney, letting me know people were still staying here. Rhosyn was arrogant to stay in the same place Alice had infiltrated to save Griffin, Ilaria's daughter, and Duchess. It felt like an eternity since that mission, but in all reality it had barely been a month.

As I stepped toward the door, Rhosyn's voice rang out, "Eumonia! It's such a surprise to see you here. Looking young again too. How odd it must be for everyone that you so favor Alice."

I stiffened as she appeared. She hadn't changed much over the years; her red hair was longer now, but otherwise, she was the same woman I'd stood side by side with a hundred and fifty-two years ago before I stepped to Earth. "Rhosyn. I've come here to ask you to stop. The game you're playing... It won't end well."

She laughed, harsh and high pitched, "You think you know the game I'm playing." She stepped closer, "You might have visions, Eu, but you have no idea what I'm truly planning."

"Why did you do it? Why pretend to be my friend? Why trap me and my people here?" I couldn't help the questions that flooded from my lips. No matter how many of my journals I analyzed, I couldn't figure out what Rhosyn truly wanted.

Mocking pity crossed her face, "You haven't figured it out yet?" My eyebrows furrowed, but she didn't give me the chance to respond. The air crackled with power, the hair on my arms rising in alarm as magick shook the ground around us. "I am Rhosyn Ivana Tenebris, granddaughter of the Red King, and I will sit upon the throne as was my right by birth."

My stomach sank, and I stumbled backwards as she launched herself at me, "Are you finally afraid, Eumonia? I hope so. I'm going to take everything from you. I'll let you live long enough for me to destroy Alice Young, just so that you die knowing your legacy will be buried and forgotten. Undraland belongs to me, and Wonderland will too very soon."

We exchanged blow for blow, spinning and ducking around each other like a sick dance. When she landed a punch hard enough to knock the wind out of me, I retreated, "Your grandfather didn't win in the end, Rhosyn, and neither will you."

With that, I turned and ran, whistling for Azura to join me. Rhosyn's laugh chased me back inside Wonderland's protective barrier. I panted as I made my way to Sammy's home in the boonies. When he opened his door, taking in my bloody visage he didn't hesitate to allow me inside. We didn't speak as he handed me warm cloths to clean myself along with bandages. I'd known Sammy his entire life, had watched him grow from a cocky young man into the tired older man that stood before me now.

"Looks like ya got yourself in a mighty big amount of trouble, ma'am. Should I be worried about who might come looking for you?" He finally asked. He set a steaming cup of tea before me, and I greedily picked it up, sipping the slightly bitter liquid.

I shook my head, "Thanks for taking care of me, Sammy. You know I'd never bring trouble directly to your door."

"Trouble always follows you Lyon women. Whether it was Cindy and Charlie, Alice and her gaggle of men, or you. I'm just glad I've been a safe place for y'all." He said, "What's the plan? Have you learned something that can help us?"

I was silent for a long time, staring into the bottom of my empty tea cup as if answers might appear. "I need you to prepare us a safe place, somewhere we can get most of the citizens safe. Ideally underground, and completely unknown... And I need you to do it without telling anyone."

Sammy watched my face for a moment before nodding, "I'll do what I can."

"You'll know when its time to start bringing people to safety." I stood, "Thank you, Sam. Your support of me and my family will never be forgotten."

He stood, pressing a kiss to my cheek, "Eumonia Lyon, remember that without you none of the rest of us would be alive. We owe you a debt that can never be repaid."

I began my trek back to Wonderland with no new answers. I didn't know what Rhosyn was planning, but I knew I had to do anything I could to protect my family from her. Wonderland had thrived for one hundred and fifty two years, I wasn't going to give up on it now.

Chapter 18

April 25ᵗʰ, 2159

I found Duchess outside, running. I watched in shock as Edik shouted out commands that made no sense to me, but with every word he said Duchess performed some new exercise. When he noticed me, he said, "Ten-minute break."

Duchess was panting as she approached me, I extended her a canteen of water that I'd brought with me. She nodded, before turning it up, drinking every drop in a matter of moments. "What are you doing?" I asked, when she handed me back my canteen.

"Edik says that my body needs discipline before my magick." Her explanation made sense, but I was still surprised. "Clearly, I have the ability to open portals. I just need to find control over it." She continued, when she saw the look on my face, "It's not that serious. None of us want to be stuck here forever."

"Thank you... for trying." I said.

"It's not just for you." She responded, "I have to get back to it."

"Why don't you join me and the guys for dinner tonight?" I rushed to ask.

She paused for a moment, glancing toward Edik, "I... Okay."

I watched for a while, unsure how I felt to see Duchess evolving past the snotty girl I knew. I walked away, more curious about her relationship with Edik, and hopeful that we might return to Wonderland soon.

Sporekin greeted me as I entered the castle, "I must... return to... my tree."

I winced at his words, taking note that none of the babies were with him, "Sporekin, I'm so sorry. The Tumtum tree was destroyed in the attack; it wouldn't be safe for you to return. You can make your home here, in the castle or on the grounds instead."

He was quiet for a moment, "The Shadelume... Queen... will not like our staying here. It encroaches on her territory."

I hadn't considered that the creatures of Undraland had their own territory, "I'll speak with her."

He nodded and loped back up the stairs without another word. Nova appeared seconds later, as if she'd heard the conversation and knew I was going to speak to her mother. She climbed up my body, resting like a scarf around my shoulders. I made my way outside to the entrance of the maze where I so often noticed Basha sunbathing. As we approached a small voice spoke into my mind, *"She rests toward the center."*

I froze, glancing around. A small purr from Nova, drew my attention downwards into her glowing blue eyes. Something nudged against my mind again, *"Until I grow, this is the best way for us to communicate."*

"That's you," I said, running a hand over her fluffy white tail that rested against my chest. She purred harder in response; she butted her head against my cheek, nuzzling me. I smiled. Nova had wormed her way into my heart, becoming one of my favorite parts of Undraland. Being able to communicate with her was exciting, *"Thank you for choosing me."*

We walked through the maze, Nova guiding me to ensure I didn't get lost in the sprawling hedges. When we reached the center, I couldn't help but look at the statues again. Queens and Kings of that past, forever frozen in time. Wyth's spot now stood empty, but as I bent down I found myself reading a plaque with Eumonia's name on it.

"They aren't just statues. They're grave markers." Basha said, startling me. I looked at the space around me with new light. A cemetery in the center of a maze. The old Kings and Queens, forever guarding the vorporal sword that now rested at my waist each day. I hadn't used it yet, but occasionally I would feel its magick reaching for me, waiting for the moment I'd need it. I opened my mouth to speak, but Basha interrupted me, "I know why you're here. Nova has already explained the Sporekin's situation."

"Will you allow them to stay here?" I asked carefully.

Basha leaned down, grooming her paw. I waited with bated breath, unsure what the Queen of the Shadelumes would say, "Undraland is dying. The Tumtum tree's loss will speed up its death. I ask you one thing, Queen... How will you save the creatures of Undraland?"

Her words were no shock to me. I was connected to this land, had been the moment I awoke here. Occasionally, I would wake in the night, Undraland's pain calling out to me. "If Duchess can open a portal, then I will invite all the creatures of Undraland to Wonderland."

"And how do you think the humans will react when they are invaded by strange creatures? How will my children adapt to a land without magick?" Basha grilled me.

I sighed, "I don't know, but it is my duty not only to protect Undraland, but to protect the citizens of Wonderland as well. I'll find a way to save everyone, I swear it."

We stared at each other for several tense moments. I could feel Basha prodding at my mind, seeking weakness. When she pulled away, she said, "The Sporekin have my blessing, but they must not enter my maze. I will not stop my people from defending our home."

"Understood. Thank you." Before I could turn to leave, Nova jumped down from her perch on my shoulder and ran to her mother. They rubbed heads, the glow of their fur brightening as they connected. I felt uncomfortable watching the intimate moment, so I said, "I'm going to return to the castle for dinner. Basha, you're welcome inside anytime."

"Why are you so nervous?" Wyth asked as I rearranged the silverware on the table a second time, "Duchess is your cousin."

"We have a complicated relationship." I sighed, smoothing the blue napkins March had found over the plate, "Without Duchess we are stranded in Undraland with no way out. That's a lot of pressure on her shoulders. I don't want to make it worse... But I need her to figure out her magick."

Wyth kissed the top of my head, "It's going to work out, beautiful. I'm sure of it." I wished I had his confidence. Instead, my magick buzzed under my skin, reacting to the anxiety that built in my gut with each day I found myself stuck in Undraland.

Hatter and March entered the dining room hand in hand, genuine smiles on their faces. It warmed my heart to see them together and so in love. They had earned the love they shared, and it brought me joy to see my husbands together. They both greeted me with a kiss.

"It looks good, Ali. When is Cheshire bringing the food up?" March asked as he took the seat next to me.

"I'm right here." Cheshire announced, causing the rest of us to jump and yelp. He cackled as he sat a steaming pot in the center of the table, "I made something like potato soup. Just... Undraland ingriendents."

"I'm sure it'll be delicious," Wyth said.

Caterpillar arrived next, taking the seat across from me without a word. As his stormy eyes a took me in, my skin flushed with heat. There was something about the way he looked at me that made me want to crawl across the table and lick every inch of his exposed skin. He smirked as if he could read my thoughts, "How was your day, princess?"

"I got Basha to agree to Sporekin living here." Wyth's eyebrows nearly met his hairline at my words. "What? Why are you looking at me like that?"

"None of the creatures of Undraland have coexisted in hundreds of years. There were tensions between the Sporekin and Shadelume long before Eumonia took the throne. It's just... you are truly special."

"Oh, we all know how special Alice is." Duchess said from the doorway, a hand already on her hip, "My mother ranted about it nightly. Alcinda's perfect, mysterious spawn."

"I didn't know that." I muttered, "Have a seat." I motioned to the open chair next to Hatter.

She stood there for a moment, staring at the empty seat. Whatever argument she had with herself seemed to play out on her features, "There's a lot that you don't know."

"Look at us, having a family dinner again." Cheshire said, "I'm starving. Let's dig in." He grabbed the bowl in front of me, dipping me a heaping spoonful of creamy white soup. I stared into the bowl contemplating Duchess' words. I'd known that Penthea had been searching for me, but I hadn't considered how much her obsession had affected her daughters life. Chatter happened around me as everyone began to eat.

"I'm sorry that I've been self-absorbed. I know you had a hard life with your parents. None of us have truly given you the space to deal with that." I blurted out several minutes later, causing the table to go silent, "It was wrong of me to assume you were the traitor, and it was wrong to me to put so much pressure on you about the magick. I know you want to go home just as bad as I do. I'm not perfect. I do know that."

Duchess stared at me, her brown eyes wide and unblinking. Her spoon hovered over her bowl, as she clearly reached for something to say, "Why didn't you invite the Knights to dinner?"

I glanced to Wyth, who responded, "I did. They don't feel... comfortable dining with their Queen yet. Ledger, Edik, and Kori are still figuring out what Knighthood will look like in these new times. I'll keep inviting them until they agree to come but... I think you should try inviting them. They might accept your invitation."

She nodded at his response, before turning her eyes back to mine, "I'm a bitch, Al. Don't take it too personally. You haven't... mistreated me that much."

I nodded, turning to eat my soup. I was surprised as familiar flavors exploded across my tongue. While a lot of things in Undraland mirrored what was available in Wonderland, they were never exactly the same. Cheshire's potato soup was almost exactly the same, creamy, cheesy, and delicious. I groaned as I took a second bite, "This is so good."

Everyone grunted their agreements, and we lapsed into silence as we all ate multiple bowls of soup. "You've got to take some to the Knights. They need this." Duchess said as she leaned back in her chair. "Kori would probably kiss you for this."

"I don't think Alice wants to share me with anyone else." Cheshire winked, "But why don't you take the rest to them. We aren't going to be able to finish it."

"I'll go with you." I said, "I need to walk some of that off." The guys glanced at me, but understood instantly that I wanted to talk to Duchess in private. I grabbed the pot, motioning for her to lead the way.

We walked toward the lower levels of the castle in silence, before Duchess suddenly said, "I don't want your guilt. I meant what I said."

"You're not... It's just... I've spent most of our relationship either trying to survive or focused on the guys. I want us to be close, we deserve that. We're family, regardless of our mother's relationship." I explained.

"I guess being related to a Queen isn't so bad." She snorted. We started down the stairs that led to the Knight's quarter, "I'm glad you have them... the guys... It's lonely in Wonderland."

I watched her profile carefully, her eyes held a far away look. "You know... You've been spending a lot of time with the Knights... Are you interested in one of them? Or all of them?"

She scoffed, "They all think I'm a spoiled, lazy brat. The only reason Edik's helping me is out of respect for you and Wyth."

I didn't think that was true, but the pink that had filled her cheeks at the suggestion gave me enough information that I didn't want to press her further. Our relationship was fragile, she didn't need me to interfere in her love life. Duchess knocked when we approached the first room. I was surprised to see Ledger open the door, his mask forgotten. His long brown hair nearly reached his ass, but what drew my attention were the deep scars carved across his face.

"What the fuck are you doing here?" He snapped, scrambling for his helmet. "Edik! Duchess is here for you."

Duchess' eyes were wide as she glanced to me. I shook my head, handing her the pot. "Ledger, I'm sorry. We didn't mean to interrupt your evening. I just wanted to share the dinner Cheshire made."

Edik and Kori appeared in the doorway, hiding Ledger from sight. "My Queen! Duchess! You are so kind. Please come in, we were just playing some cards. You're more than welcome to join us."

"Oh. Are you sure?" Duchess asked.

"I'm sorry gentlemen. I can't tonight, but I will ask for a rain check very soon." I said, "Duchess, please, enjoy your evening. Thanks for joining us for dinner." I nearly sprinted away, taking the stairs two at a time before anyone could respond. Just because I didn't want to interfere, didn't mean I wouldn't encourage Duchess to chase the Knights any chance I got.

Chapter 19

April 29th, 2159

I was on edge. The air of the castle was thick with tension, suffocating me slowly. An energy hung heavy, dark, and looming. The suns had not shone as brightly for the last few days. There had been no new attacks, no stirrings in Undraland, but something under my skin could not find peace. I'd paced until my legs ached, I couldn't focus on reading, and I couldn't leave the castle at night. Not with the Noxroots lurking closer and closer to the ground. Not with the Queen of Hearts, who could pop into Undraland at any moment, with her monstrous beast...

"Alice." Caterpillar's stern voice pulled me from my spiraling thoughts. "You're leaking magick." He nodded to my hands; they glowed silver, but the danger was in the electricity that had formed all around them, snapping at anything close to me.

I leaned against the wall, sinking to the floor. I couldn't form words, my stress and anxiety stealing my voice away. Before tears could start rolling down my face, Caterpillar was on his knees pulling me into his arms without a word. "Stop holding it back, princess. I'm here, and I'll take care of you." It was all the permission I needed to break down. With Caterpillar I knew I didn't have to be strong, I didn't even have to control the magick that flooded through my system thanks to his void abilities. So, I cried, I screamed, and I unleashed all of the emotions I'd spent weeks stuffing away just to survive. Caterpillar didn't waiver for a moment, holding me tightly.

As quickly as the panic had begun it sapped away, leaving me red eyed and embarrassed at my breakdown.

"I'm sorry." I said, pulling away.

"No." He grunted, "You are not going to apologize for having feelings. I will turn you over my knee if I have to, to make you understand that while everyone else might look to you as their Queen, you are my wife first. I will always be here to hold you when you need to cry."

I sniffed, "I love you, Roman."

"I love you too," He stood, helping me to my feet, "Now, why don't we go down to the kitchen and have a hot cup of weird tea?"

I nodded, letting him lead me down to the kitchen in silence. He motioned for me to sit at the small table that was tucked into the corner. I stared down at the dark wood grain, imagining the staff that would have sat here hundreds of years ago while serving my ancestors. What were their lives like under Eumonia or her parents? It was still hard for me to imagine the castle bustling with magick users. I wanted to live in a world where the magick users were safe to exist in the same way as the humans. I'd started that in Wonderland, but I still saw the way my people were treated. Like prized pigs or pariahs. While most citizens respected me, they didn't extend that respect to the other magick users. Even though they had been enslaved by the Red Queen for forty years. Could I bring them here? Give all magick users the life they truly deserved in Undraland?

Caterpillar once again pulled me from my thoughts, this time with a steaming cup of dark brown liquid. We had been calling it tea, but it was more bitter, not quite coffee, but some strange mix of the two. I took a sip before asking, "If we can defeat the Queen of Hearts, how would you feel about living in Undraland?"

I watched his face, hoping to see his response before he spoke, but he didn't react to the question. "You like it here." He observed, "Whether he wants to admit it or not, so does March. He's been crocheting more than I've ever seen before, or playing with the Burrowyn he befriended. Cheshire and Hatter are harder to read, but obviously, this is Wyth's home."

When he trailed off, I furrowed my brows, "You didn't answer my question. I wanted to hear how *you* felt about it."

He snorted, "I'm going wherever you are, Alice. I don't care if its Wonderland, Undraland, or some other world you want to fall into. It doesn't matter to me where we live or what responsibilities we have, because being with you, beside you, is the only thing that has made my life worth living." He was silent for a moment, and we both sipped on our tea, "Did you know right before Hatter saved you from the Red Party, I had been seriously considering jumping on my bike and riding straight out of Wonderland?" I shook my head, surprised at the information. He had seemed so dedicated to the Resistance, "Well I had been for a long time. I didn't see a way for us to win against the Red Party. The only reason I didn't leave was Hatter, March, and Cheshire. They were my responsibility; I couldn't just abandon them."

"I'm glad you didn't leave," I said, grabbing his hand. It was warm and so much larger than my own. I marveled at the dark black letters that had been tattooed across his knuckles. Rise. And he had risen. Had died and come back to me.

"I am too, Alice," He gripped my chin, forcing me to look into his grey eyes, "I will do anything you want to do. Undraland, Wonderland, none of it is the same for me if you aren't there. The weeks that we were apart felt like an eternity. You're not leaving my side again."

I was up and crawling into his lap in seconds. His words lit a passion in me that could not be denied. This was my husband, my Caterpillar, my Roman Ainsworth. Our lips met in fiery collision, devouring and all-consuming. I moaned as his hands slid down my body, removing all of my clothing in seconds. When I was bare before him, he pulled away, holding me in place as he took me in, "Creator, you drive me crazy." He tweaked my hard nipples, before grabbing my hips and turning me around. I gasped as I found Wyth standing in the door, shirtless, every one of his rippling muscles on display.

He coughed, slightly, "I'm sorry to interrupt."

"Get over here." Caterpillar commanded, "We are her heartmates, we'll take her together."

My eyes widened, but the idea had me clinching my thighs together, "Please, Wyth?"

His swirling eyes blew black with lust as he made his way to us. Caterpillar stood, "I'm taking her ass." Wyth nodded his agreement, before shoving the linen pant he wore down to his feet. He kicked them away as he picked me up and slide into my pussy in one movement, forcing a scream from my throat.

"Shh, shh, my heart. You don't want to wake anyone." Wyth said as he fucked me slowly. When I felt Caterpillar's cock press against my ass, I pushed back eagerly, desperate to be filled by both of them. Caterpillar grabbed my hips, forcing me to be still as he pressed deeper into me. The feeling of being held and filled by both of them was enough to have my legs shaking. They found a rhythm that brought tears to my eyes.

"That's my good girl, taking us so well. Is this what you needed?" Caterpillar murmured into my ear. One of his hands drifted from my side, finding my clit with ease.

"Yes!" I cried as he brought me to an eye-watering orgasm. Pleasure zipped down my spine, the glow of my skin growing brighter with every additional thrust. Wyth groaned first, gripping my hips harder enough to bruise as he filled me with his seed. Caterpillar pounded into me harder, hands masterfully playing with my nipples, prolonging my orgasm until he grunted, finishing in my ass with one final, punishing thrust.

We carefully disentangled, but Wyth swept me into his arms the moment he pulled his pants back on, "A hot bath and sleep."

He nodded to Caterpillar, who kissed my head, "I'll clean up down here. Get some rest, princess. We are here to take care of you in every way that you need."

I rested my head against Wyth's shoulder as he carried me to his room. We didn't speak until he had tucked me into bed, my head resting over his heart. "I didn't expect to ever share you with your other husbands. Is that something you do often?"

I quirked a brow, "My other husbands? Is this your way of proposing?"

"A heartmate is a deeper bond than husband and wife. The moment I laid eyes on you in the maze after you had stabbed me with the vorporal sword, you became my world." He responded seriously, "But that did not answer my question."

"Yes, we often... enjoy group activities." Heat suffused my cheeks at the images that rushed through my mind, "In time, I'm sure you will as well... If you want to."

"I'm intrigued by the idea of seeing you take all of us at once." He said. Wyth was always so matter of fact, I loved it. "But not yet. I need to grow closer with all of your husbands."

"I'm glad to see you and Caterpillar have bonded." I pressed a kiss to his chest. Sleep hung heavy behind my eyes, and I yawned.

"Sleep, my heart." Wyth whispered, and as if he'd used magick, I began to drift off into a blissfully dreamless sleep.

Chapter 20

⁕⁕⁕⁕⁕ ⁕⁕⁕⁕⁕

Duchess

April 30th, 2159

I couldn't help the grunt of frustration that left my throat as the small portal I'd been trying to summon fizzled out before me. "You cannot allow your mind to drift away from the task at hand. Close your eyes, again." Edik chastised from behind me.

I sat cross-legged in the gardens behind the castle, everyone milled around, trying to pretend that they weren't watching me fail over and over again. Alice sat in a chair, the two suns overhead shining down on her perfect platinum blonde hair. Hatter and March laughed at something she said, and a wave of jealousy rolled through me. It wasn't that I wanted her life, I wasn't stupid enough to believe she had an easy life, but the easy love she shared with the men who adored her? I craved it more than I could ever admit.

"She can't do it, Edik. I don't see why you're wasting your time." Ledger's voice set me on edge. I could tell he hated me, not just his words, but the way he avoided me no matter what. He'd barely acknowledged my existence when I'd joined them for cards.

"I'd like to see you try." I snapped back, standing. "Oh wait. You can't, because I'm one of two people with this ability."

"It was wasted on you." Ledger spat, "A useless, spoiled girl."

Rage stirred in me, but something else followed. Shame, bone deep. I needed to master my magick, had been trying for weeks, but I'd made no progress. I was useless. We were trapped here, because I couldn't summon a portal for more than a few mere seconds. My life was better before Rhosyn had forced my magick to the surface.

"Ledger, just... leave her alone." Kori said, before turning to me, "Can I make a suggestion?" He looked to Edik. Edik nodded, motioning toward me, "You've been meditating right?" I nodded. Edik had made meditation part of my training. Something about the brain being a muscle that also had to be trained. Kori approached, laying a hand against my chest, "Magick doesn't come from the mind, it resides in the heart. Sit back down," He ordered, "Close your eyes. Imagine your magick, find its warmth inside of you." I followed his instruction, but as I tried to reach inward, I found nothing but darkness. Emptiness. I was an empty shell. A failure, "Stop. You're thinking too much. Just feel, let the magick come to you."

We continued like that for what felt like hours. I'd clear my mind, hoping to feel the spark of my magick, but nothing manifested. Finally, I threw my hands in the air, "This isn't working."

Wyth approached at my shout, "May I try something?"

"I am not everyone's science experiment." I snapped, unable to stop myself. My shame and frustration warred inside of me, causing me to lash out.

"No, you are my heartmate's family. I only want to help you both return to your home." His voice was gentle, like he was trying to calm an angry child.

"Fine, whatever." He held out his hands, his beautiful face serene, waiting for me. I placed my hands in his.

"My primary magick is of a similar vein to Alice's. I can amplify and direct any form of magick that exists. I am going to help you connect with your magick." I tensed as I felt his magick gently prodding at my mind.

"Just relax and allow me in." That was easier said than done, but I forced myself to follow his direction. His magick was like a cool cloth against my heated neck, and I found my shoulders relaxing. I could feel the way it prodded around inside me, but it didn't feel like an invasion. I tensed when I felt something niggling against the center of my chest. "Duchess, breathe. I've found a blockage, I'm going to try to remove it." Pain flared through me as I felt his magick rip away the cap that rested over my magick. My heart raced, my breathing hitched as magick flooded through my entire body. It vibrated beneath my skin painfully, as if my body was too small to withstand its power.

My eyes flew open, frantically searching for help, instead of Wyth's face only darkness surrounded me.

"Vivica Rose, the blood that flows through your veins, has wreaked havoc upon my world. Tell me why I should allow you the power that has been locked away within you for so long." The voice that rang around me was impossible to describe. It boomed in my ears, disorienting me even further, *"Answer me, daughter."*

"I need it to get home. To help Alice." I cried out, collapsing to my knees as the pain of my magick awakening became too much. *"I swear I'm not like my parents. I just... I want to be happy."* I whispered.

"Do you know who I am?" The voice was less angry now, allowing me to hear the softer, feminine notes of its speech.

"The Creator." I breathed, *"I'll swear any oath you require, but please allow me to access my magick. It's the only way for Alice to return home."* The Creator didn't respond right away, allowing me a chance to recover. I stood up, smoothing out the clothes I wore. Simple, linen. Nothing like what I would have worn in Wonderland. Yet I'd come to love the fabric here; it was so different from what I wore, but it felt right. Undraland felt right. I hadn't wanted to admit it, but I'd come to enjoy life here. Even as I struggled, the beauty of this world wasn't lost on me. The strange singing flowers Kori had spent an hour describing to me after I found them in a

children's book, the deep red sky at night, the way no one looked at me with disdain or pity.

"You love my world." The Creator observed, breaking the silence I'd grown used to. Darkness may have surrounded me, but I was more comfortable in darkness than I ever had been in the light. *"I will grant you the power you require, Vivica Rose, but know that if you ever betray my Champion or Undraland, I will ensure you learn pain the same way your mother did."*

The darkness began to fade, and my ears were ringing as the faces around me came into focus. Alice kneeled above me, the suns haloed around her, "Are you okay? You passed out after Wyth unlocked the block on your magick."

I sat up, blinking against the bright light. I glanced down at my hands, feeling my full magick for the first time. I held out my hand, summoning a portal. It no longer felt like a struggle, the swirling black void appeared seconds later. I jumped up, throwing myself headlong through it. It felt like moving through warm liquid, but when I stepped through the other side I found myself across the lawn from where I'd been standing before. "It fucking worked!" I shouted, causing everyone to turn toward me with shock on their faces. "I finally did it!"

Alice grinned, "Does that mean it's time to go home?"

I nodded, "Get your shit together, we're going back to Wonderland!" Alice and her men cheered before heading back to the castle to gather their things. Only the Knights remained, a sense of uncertainty seeming to hold them in place. "You know y'all can come with us if you want to."

Edik shook his head, "It is our duty to protect Undraland. We've already decided to stay. I hope... I hope you and the Queen return to us soon."

I ignored the strange taste of sadness that caught in my throat, "Thank you... for helping me. It really did make a difference."

"It has been my pleasure... Our pleasure, Vivica." The sound of his voice saying my name sent a shiver down my spine. I took that as my cue to leave.

Whatever feelings I had for Edik… or Kori didn't matter. I wasn't ready for a relationship, and they'd never shown any real interest. It was a dream I could not indulge in.

Night had fallen while everyone was preparing to leave Undraland. We stood in the center of the maze. Wyth had insisted this was the usual place to portal from. I ignored the way the statue of my long-dead family members seemed to watch me. Alice stood upfront, Nova wrapped around her neck like a scarf. The Shadelume Queen had already said her goodbyes, disappearing from our sight one final time. The Knights stood behind us, Wyth had gripped each of their helmets, resting his head against them in some form of goodbye that I did not understand.

"Ready?" Alice asked, joining me in the center of the maze.

I swallowed hard, "As I'll ever be. I'm going to try to drop us in the center of the city."

"You got this, Duchess, but I'm right here if you need help." She said, before stepping away.

I closed my eyes, calling the magick that rested just under my heart. It responded in an instant, warmth filling my palms as I wove the portal before me. I imagined the statue that had looked over the city of Wonderland for so long. Sweat formed on my brow as I focused all of my magick and energy on widening and reinforcing the portal.

When I finally opened my eyes, the swirling black vortex was large enough for two people to walk through at a time. I turned slightly, "Time to give it a try."

Alice stepped forward, but Hatter and March grabbed her, forcing her behind them. They stepped through first, and I could feel them slip through to the other side. Alice and Caterpillar went next. I was surprised when Roman gave me a nod of respect. Wyth stopped next to me, "We can go through together."

I shook my head, "You'll have to go first."

He looked back at his Knights, an unreadable look on his face, "May the Creator be with you." He said, before stepping through the portal as well.

I turned to look back at the Knights, "Last chance to join us in Wonderland, boys."

"Maybe next time," Kori shouted back, "Be safe and well, Vivica Rose."

"Stop doubting yourself so much." Edik said, "The Creator is always with you."

Considering the conversation I'd had with the Creator, I didn't know if that brought me the kind of peace it did him. I wagged my fingers at Ledger, "Lighten up."

His grunt was the last thing I heard before I allowed the portal to take me.

Portal travel was disorienting at first, when I landed in Wonderland my eyes couldn't adjust. My head spun as the sights and sounds seemed to grow around me. Strong hands on my biceps caused me to turn frantically.

"Duchess, it's me," Hatter's voice was panicked, "You have to follow me. It isn't safe out here."

"What? What's going on?" I blinked, glancing around. I gasped as I was finally able to take in the sights. Buildings were on fire all around us. Shrill screams filled the streets. Gunshots could be heard in the distance, and unidentified crashes echoed all around us. But the most disturbing sound was a beastly roar that filled the air.

Hatter dragged me along, toward our apartment building, I realized. Cheshire and March ran around the group, helping anyone they could. Alice and Caterpillar fought with magick, swords, and fists as men dressed in blood red tried to stop us. We didn't stop, pushing our way through the crowds until we arrived at our building. I was surprised to find it still standing, until I saw the golden shield that surrounded it. Alice pushed through the magick, throwing open the door so we could all fall inside. We were all covered in blood, ash, and dirt, but we'd made it here alive.

Finally, reality began to sink in. The Queen of Hearts had managed to take Wonderland, and we had arrived too late to save it.

PART THREE: SILVER QUEEN

Chapter 21

Alice

I burst into the conference room, every eye turning to take in my panting visage. My mother was the first one out of her seat, throwing herself into my arms with a sob. "You're alive." She cried, "I've been so worried."

I patted her back, taking a moment to enjoy the warmth and strength of her hug. But it didn't last long, I pulled back, "What's going on? The city is in complete chaos."

"The Queen of Hearts and the Suits have been gaining power ever since you disappeared. It became worse when the guys disappeared; the citizens lost trust in us when we couldn't meet their demands. Now..." Mom trailed off, a single tear running down her face, "Lily reinforced the building, but her shield won't last forever. Idalia has been gathering magick users and any citizens willing to trust her and bringing them here."

Rab stepped forward, embracing Caterpillar, "I'm glad to see that you're back. I'm sorry we failed to keep things peaceful."

"It's not your fault. The only person to blame is Rhosyn." I growled, "Do we know where she is?"

Sammy was the one to respond, "Eumonia left to confront Rhosyn about an hour ago."

"Alone?" I rolled my eyes. None of us were powerful enough to defeat her on our own. I had to help Eumonia. "I'm going back out there. She can't end the Queen of Hearts alone. Caterpillar-"

"No. I know what you're going to say, and I am not staying here while you go out there to risk your life." He interrupted me, "Wyth and I will go with you. Hatter, March, and Cheshire can stay here and help coordinate."

"Who is Wyth?" Tally squeaked from her position between Cahir and Jackson. Blood was smeared across her forehead, her arm in a sling. She looked shaken in a way I'd never seen from the smaller woman, whatever help she'd been for the Resistance to this point was clearly no longer an option.

Wyth stepped fully into the room, towering over everyone else. "I am Wyth, Emerald King of Undraland, friend to Eumonia. Alice is my heartmate."

Cheshire snorted, "He just said a lot of words that don't mean much to you. He's Alice's final husband, chosen by magick... or maybe the Creator. I wasn't clear on that. He's basically an alien."

"Doesn't that make us aliens t-too?" March chimed in, "Since we're magick users as well."

Cheshire hummed, "I have always felt better than everyone else."

Caterpillar rolled his eyes with a heavy sigh, "We've got to go. I want you to start organizing anyone who is in fighting shape. We're going to need soldiers out there saving innocents."

Everyone nodded. I lifted Nova from around my shoulders, "I need you to stay here where it is safe."

"*I can help you.*" Her small voice echoed through my mind.

"I promised Basha I would do everything I could to protect you. Please stay here with my mom. I'll be okay." I ignored the strange looks I got from everyone as I spoke to Nova. When a huff left her I knew I'd won the argument. I handed her to mom, "This is Nova. She and I are bonded. It's a long story; will you please watch over her?"

Mom ran her fingers over her soft white fur, "Be safe out there, Ali. I just got you back, don't leave me again."

I knew I couldn't promise her anything. Just getting here had been a fight, I didn't know what we would find when we tried to hunt down Eumonia and Rhosyn, but I couldn't let Eumonia fight the Queen of Hearts alone. I was certain the Creator wanted me to end Rhosyn myself.

Wyth and Caterpillar flanked me as we exited the building. Nothing had changed since we'd made it inside, smoke hung heavy in the air, screams and the sounds of buildings crumbling overshadowed our voices. I glanced around before making a decision, "We need to ride."

Caterpillar nodded, "Wyth is riding with you though."

I snorted, before leading Wyth toward the garage that held are bikes. Caterpillar tossed me two helmets, and I turned toward my giant, "Put this on. It'll protect your head if we crash."

"Are we going to crash?" He asked, eyeing my sleek, black bike with concern, "What is that thing?"

"This is a motorcycle... It's sort of like... Did you have anything you ride for transportation in Undraland?" I realized I'd only ever seen every one walk.

"Gryphons before the illness began and they disappeared into the mountains." He explained, "Is it fueled with magick?"

Caterpillar stepped in, "It uses gas, and we need to go. Just put the helmet on and climb on behind Alice." He checked the security of my helmet before climbing onto his own bike and revving the engine. As I climbed on a sigh of relief ran through me. I had missed riding through the streets of Wonderland. Wyth hot body pressed against mine was a welcome distraction as we drove through Wonderland. Every street was complete chaos, bodies and debris were scattered everywhere. It would take years to repair all the damage that had been done. Rage began to build in me with every new horror we witnessed.

A beast's roar rattled through my body, my magick reacted, buzzing and recoiling beneath my skin. I veered my bike toward the sound without a second thought. We rode out of the city, toward the suburbs where I'd grown up. The streets were deserted, but the homes were all in a state of disrepair. Clearly the Queen had begun her destruction. here. As we approached my childhood home, my body tensed. The home my parents had raised us in was now smoldering ashes, completely obliterated. I didn't let myself stop, speeding past with only a fleeting glance at the world that had been torn away from me by the Red Queen.

As we continued to ride, I realized where we were headed. The moment the wildflower field came into sight, my heart stopped in my chest. A massive beast, easily the size of two of the largest buildings in Wonderland, was chained to a tree. Its violet scales were stark against the greens and browns that surrounded it. Massive wings tipped with vicious-looking claws flapped hard as it strained to break free from its chains. As we moved closer, I noticed the scars covering its two legs, whip marks if I had to guess. I wanted to feel pity for it, but as we approached, it turned its head, revealing the black fangs that filled its mouth.

"The Jabberwock should not be here." Wyth whispered, "It eats magick, it'll starve on Earth."

Before Caterpillar or I could consider what he'd told us, screams erupted nearby. We turned, finally noticing Rhosyn. Her usually tamed red curls were a mess, tangled around her head, and blood dripped down her arm from a wound at her shoulder. She didn't seem to notice us, as she swung the blade she held at someone who was out of our sight. I ran without thinking, barely skirting the snapping jaws of the Jabberwock.

A blonde woman stood before Rhosyn, rage and pain painted across her face. Blood covered her, dripping onto the ground as she approached Rhosyn with her sword held high. It took me a moment to process the strange resemblance I shared with the woman, but as Wyth joined me, he growled, "Eumonia needs our help."

I glanced at Caterpillar, who shrugged, "Her appearance was an illusion."

I nodded, pulling the Vorporal blade from where it rested at my hip, but before I could rush to assist Eumonia the sounds of a tree crashing drew my attention. The Jabberwock roared as it was released from the chains that had held it in place. Its pure white eyes turned to me, and I had almost no time to stumble away as it attacked, teeth snapping against air as it tried to take a bite from me.

I ran toward the tree line, hoping to get away from it, but Caterpillar screamed, "Alice!" I turned to find the beast with its mouth agape, white light building in its throat. Seconds before it would have engulfed me entirely, I was thrown out of the way, my back slamming against a tree. A female scream pierced my eardrums as my sword fell from my grasp.

When I was back on my feet, Rhosyn was mounting the beast, a wild grin painted across her face. When her eyes met mine, she said, "We'll be meeting again soon, Little Lyon."

Before I could react, the Jabberwock launched into the sky, disappearing from sight as soon it entered the clouds. I stood there for a moment dumbfounded, before Caterpillar shouted my name. I turned, finding him and Wyth kneeling over Eumonia. I rushed to her side, falling to my knees. Her skin was blistered and red, as if she'd been sunburned, but the more shocking thing was the way her hair had turned completely white.

She let out a rasping breath, her hand squeezing mine as she struggled to speak, "You've returned... I'm so sorry I failed to protect... Wonderland. Our city needs you."

Tears spilled down my face, "We'll get you to Mom, heal you. You'll live."

Wyth shook his head. I saw the unshed tears shining in his eyes as he said, "The Jabberwock took the magick from her body, my heart. She cannot live without it. It stole away her immortality."

"No. No. I'll give her some of my magick," I called my magick to the surface, letting it reach for Eumonia. I found nothing but a dark void as I tried to reach inside of her. No matter how hard I tried no magick would take root in her. I sobbed, "Thank you. Thank you for saving my life, for giving Wonderland a chance to thrive. None of us would be here today without you." I spoke, a hand rested on the top of her head.

Her breathing became more labored, her eyes shutting as her body seemed to shake from the effort. Wyth placed a kiss on her forehead, "Queen Eumonia Lyon, you have served Undraland and Wonderland faithfully for long enough. Join the Creator and be at peace."

Tears and snot ran down my face unchecked. I had grown to see Eumonia like the grandmother I'd never had. We had not known each other long, but she had been watching over me and my family for hundreds of years. As the final breath left her body, something shifted in my chest. Rage and determination hardening, sharpening. I stood, moving to pick up the Vorporal sword from where it had fallen when Eumonia had sacrificed her life for me.

I turned back to Caterpillar and Wyth as they carefully lifted Eumonia's limp body, "That bitch will die a thousand deaths by my hand. The last thing she'll see before I cut her fucking head off is my face."

They both nodded. "She should be buried in Undraland, where all the Lyon's that came before her rest." Wyth said.

"I'll speak with Duchess. We can travel freely now, she'll be honored in the way that she deserves." Caterpillar responded.

I couldn't speak as they planned how to get her body home. My grief had turned my tongue to lead. Too many people had died on my behalf, too many at the hands of the power-hungry beasts that still roamed through my worlds. I was going to put an end to it. No matter what the cost was.

Chapter 22

May 2nd, 2159

Even with Wonderland in disarray, I insisted that we could not wait to give Eumonia the burial she deserved in Wonderland. Mom, Sammy, Rab, Lily, and Idalia gawked as they recovered from traveling through the portal. The Knights stood as sentries as Caterpillar, Wyth, Hatter, and Cheshire carried the white coffin we had managed to find to the freshly opened grave. March held my hand, my rock, as tears rolled down my face. Once they reached the hole, carefully setting Eumonia coffin into its final resting place, everyone but Wyth joined me.

"We are here today to honor the life of Queen Eumonia Selene Lyon. For over one hundred and eighty years, she served Undraland faithfully, even while trapped a world away. Her power and legacy will forever be honored." Wyth's voice echoed around us, and the hedges began to rustle. Basha and Sporekin appeared, followed by a small herd of Burrowyn. A caw overhead drew my attention to Azura. She landed on the coffin, a shrill, sad sound leaving her. I wasn't sure how she'd followed us into Undraland, but I decided not to worry about it. I walked up, extending my arm. After she was perched on my shoulder, each of the creatures of Undraland stepped forward to pay their respects. Sporekin tore a small piece from his beard, dropping it on top of the casket with words that none of us could understand. Basha followed, dropping a branch covered in tiny yellow flowers from her mouth, Nova rushed to her side, and together they keened. A large Burrowyn flew to the edge of the coffin, depositing what looked like leaves atop it.

I stepped forward next, taking the roses that Mom had brought with her. I dropped them atop the coffin, and turned to the small crowd, "Eumonia watched over me and my family for our entire lives. She sacrificed everything to give us the best chance at a life in Wonderland, even when she'd lost everything and everyone she cared for." I sniffed, unable to hold back the emotions I felt, "It is my duty to her to save Wonderland and Undraland. I will not stop until Rhosyn pays for what she has done."

I returned to Hatter, who immediately pulled me into his arms, pressing a kiss to the top of my head. Sammy stepped forward, surprising me, "Most of y'all don't know this, but I have known Eumonia my entire life. She spent much of her time in the boonies, caring for the less fortunate. She was a truly kind soul, who put the needs of others above her own at every turn. We will all suffer for having lost her presence in our world." He turned, pulling a blue handkerchief from his pocket. He leaned down carefully, placing it with the rest of the items upon Eumonia's coffin. Once he had shuffled back to us, tears shining in his eyes, the knights moved forward.

Wyth nodded to them, and I watched in fascination as the four of them began to glow. Green and gold magick flared brighter as the ground moved, covering the coffin as if the hole had never been opened. Wyth said, "Creator, may Queen Eumonia's soul find comfort in your arms." The knights echoed his words before the magick guttered out.

As soon as the grave was closed, the Burrowyn fled back through the hedge. Sporekin and Basha shared a nod before Sporekin bowed at the waist to me and hurried away. Basha approached my mother and said, "I've heard whispers of a White Queen in Wonderland, the Queen that Never Was."

"I never wanted a throne, just peace for myself and my daughter," Mom responded, kneeling before the Shadelume without fear, "You are Basha, Queen of the Shadelumes, Nova's mother?"

I could see the pride in Basha's stance, "I am. No Shadelume has traveled between worlds as my daughter has. The Silver Queen and the Shadelume Princess will have stories written about them for centuries to come."

It took a moment for me to realize the Silver Queen was a moniker for me. But as it sunk in, something about it felt... final. As if I was slowly accepting my role as Queen. I didn't know what the future would hold, but I was never going to allow someone to die in my place again.

May 3ʳᵈ, 2159

Everyone was exhausted. Traveling to Undraland for Eumonia's funeral while continuing to save anyone we could find from the chaos that still rained down on the city had drained me. I sat on the couch, appreciating the off-white paint of our walls, when the door suddenly opened. A man I'd never seen before burst in. He froze when he saw me, "Ah... I am sorry. I was looking for Maxton." The man was slightly disheleved in a pale-yellow sweater and jean, his brown hair didn't look like it had been combed in days. I instantly realized I was looking at March's father. Their resemblance was undeniable.

I stood, "He should be back in a few minutes, him and Hatter went to help the new arrivals settle into the basement." We were running out of space, and Cheshire and Idalia couldn't handle everyone's complaints alone any longer. We were going to have to find a new safe place soon, or we'd have riots on our hands.

"You must be Alice. Max has told me so much about you, I'm glad to finally have the chance to meet you. My name is Henry." He offered me his hand, and I shook it quickly before motioning for him to sit.

"March told me the magick users named you, The Poet. You saved a lot of lives during the Red Queen's reign. Why didn't you approach me when I freed everyone else?" I asked. Maybe it was rude to be so direct, but something about the story March had told me didn't feel entirely right.

He glanced the left, shifting nervously in his chair. "Truthfully, I wanted to wait and see what you would do." When I lifted a brow, he sighed, "Magick users have always been vital to Wonderland's functionality. I wanted to see exactly what you would ask of them. If you had turned out to be like the Red Queen, I wanted to have the power of anonymity."

"But you left your young son with me." I pointed out.

"I was fearful. His mother was dead, I'd already failed one of my children. If you turned out to be corrupt, I had hoped that I could save him before you realized our connection. That night... in the dungeon... You seemed so genuine. I was desperate." Henry's explanation made enough sense, even if I could not imagine leaving my young child with someone I didn't trust.

March, Cheshire, and Hatter rushing into the room stopped our conversation, "Alice, can you come down? The magick users and the... humans..." Cheshire trailed off, "It feels weird to say I'm not human. Sorry."

"What Cheshire is trying to say is that tensions are at an all time high. March couldn't get through to everyone, would you mind to give it a try." Hatter said.

"I'll go too." Henry offered, "If you don't mind of course." He turned to me, sheepishly.

I nodded, following the guys to the basement. Before we had even opened the doors, I could hear the tension in the raised voices. There was easily three hundred people crammed into the gym that had been converted into a safe house. Cots were spaced as close together as they could be while still allowing people room to navigate. A line had formed leading into the showers. The room seemed to be split, a group of about a hundred people were tucked into the back corner. A few I recognized, so I beelined to them. As soon as they noticed me, they perked up, "I hear we're having some issues. I know it's a tight squeeze down here, I promise we are all working to come up with a better option to keep everyone safe."

A few of the regular citizens had noticed me and wandered over. "How are you planning to fix all the destruction outside?" One man shouted.

It was a symphony of complaints from there. Everyone began to shout their grievances at once, making my head ache. Before I could open my mouth to try to calm them down, Henry jumped onto one of the cots, a sharp whistle leaving his mouth. "I know we're all tired, hungry, and angry, but shouting and fighting will get us nowhere." I could feel the magick he was weaving as he spoke, "Do not let the Queen of Hearts win through your desperation. We have suffered before. We can survive anything that is thrown our way, so long as we stand together against the rule of those who want us under their boot."

Several people cheered as the magick he had woven seeped in. I stepped forward, "We are working to get more food down here within the hour. We will not stop until everyone is safe and the Queen of Hearts can no longer cause chaos in Wonderland."

Everyone slowly returned to what they had been doing, magick still lingering in the area. When Henry returned to my side, I patted his shoulder, "Thank you. I'm impressed. Most of the magick users aren't as well trained as you."

"My magick is easier to control than most. I'll stay with them, keep the peace until you've come up with a better solution." He gave me a small smile, "You're a good woman, Alice Young. My son is very lucky to have you at his back."

"I'm luckier to have him at mine." I glanced to where March was kneeling before a small girl. He held a small doll in his long fingers, carefully sewing a tear along the doll's back. The tension that had been coiled inside him since we'd met seemed to have disappeared. A new sense of confidence and belonging taking its place.

Hatter joined us, wrapping an arm around me. Henry disappeared into the crowd, and I glanced up seeing a smile playing across Hatter's face. When he noticed my stare he said, "I know I shouldn't be happy with everything going on, but seeing March finally accepting who he is without shame... I never thought I'd see the day."

"Neither did I." Hatter's father, Joshua, chimed in from behind us.

"Dad, I haven't seen you since we got back. Where have you been hiding?" Hatter asked.

"Alcinda asked me to help the more traumatized members of our refuges. Some of these people have been through hell. I don't know what that woman is doing, but she has to be stopped." He explained.

"We're doing what we can. If you hear any information that you think might be helpful, will you let us know?" I asked.

"Of course." He turned to me, "I'm... glad you are okay, Alice."

"Thank you, Joshua. If you need any help with the survivors, please let me know." I kissed Hatter on the cheek, glancing to see Cheshire trying to blend into the wall, "I'm going to get Ches out of here before he decides to go invisible permanently."

Cheshire didn't complain as I dragged him from the basement. When we entered the apartment, I beelined straight to his cave. Once we were safely inside, he exhaled deeply, before heading directly to his computer. "I've been tracing the attacks looking for some kind of pattern. If we could catch her team maybe we can end them."

"Cheshire, you need to take a deep breath." I grabbed the mouse from his hand, "You do this every time there's a crisis. I saw how much you relaxed in Undraland, you weren't burdened by all of this." I motioned to the screens of his computer.

"Do you regret coming back?" He asked, but I saw the guilt in his navy blue eyes as soon as the words left his lips. "Sorry, I shouldn't-"

"Yeah I do." I interrupted him, "Wonderland isn't Wonderland anymore. It doesn't feel... like home. I missed my people not this place."

"We can't just abandon the citizens though." He pointed out. "They are innocent."

"And we won't, but... I've been thinking... Once the Queen of Hearts is gone, maybe we should have Duchess open a portal. Give everyone a choice. Stay here or go with us." I admitted. I had breathed easier during Eumonia's funeral. As if the air in Undraland had become integral to my being. Undraland wasn't perfect, but I had felt more at home in my few weeks there than I ever had in Wonderland.

"I'd like that." He breathed, resting his head against my chest, "A life with you in the castle, seeing you become the Queen you were always meant to be... That's what I want. I might even grow used to the lack of tech with all the strange creatures to befriend."

"Maybe we can find a way to make your tech work there." I laughed, as if admitting how much I wanted to return to Undraland had lifted a weight from my chest. "But first, why don't we just watch a movie or something. You can fill me in on the pattern later, when Caterpillar and Wyth return."

"Have I mentioned how much I love you, Al?" Cheshire asked.

"I could stand to hear it more." I said, laughing as he captured my lips with his. Even in the worst moments of my life Sinclair Malone found a way to make me laugh. We kept each other smiling, making all the pain and suffering we had seen a little easier to bare.

Chapter 23

May 5th, 2159

I'd learned to wear earplugs when we were out in the districts. It was impossible to distinguish conversation over the sounds of screams and buildings collapsing. Rhosyn had not stopped her assault on Wonderland, growing bolder with each new attack she launched. She seemed hellbent on annihilating the entire city. Lily's shield was holding strong, but I could see the strain it was taking on her. Her usual golden braid had grown lackluster, dark bags developing under her eyes. She had been tasked with staying with Lewis and Caroline while the rest of us ventured into the city.

The guys and I moved through the streets as a single unit, clearing buildings and gathering survivors any chance we could. I slowed as a familiar shock of blue hair caught my eyes. I rushed to see that Sheridan had collapsed several feet away from the entrance to her parents restaurant. It had been vandalized, windows smashed, the sign that had once held my name now a charred mess on the ground.

"Are you okay?" I asked, as I kneeled beside her. Her eyes were red and puffy as if she'd been crying for hours.

"She took them... But I... I felt the moment they..." She broke down sobbing. "The Queen of Hearts killed my parents after she drained their magick." I flinched at the words, instantly knowing she'd taken Clinton and Sara to feed the Jabberwock.

"I'm so sorry, Sheridan." I choked out, past the lump that had formed in my throat. "Please come with us. We will keep you safe."

Her eyes met mine, hardening, "Will you kill her?"

I froze, but nodded, "For your parents and everyone else she's taken from us all."

"Make sure she suffers." She said, before standing.

Caterpillar escorted her to Idalia's van before I could say anything else. "She's strong. She'll recover." Wyth said, laying a hand on my shoulder, "It is not your fault that Rhosyn is harming these people."

"She's targeting them on purpose, because they named their diner after me. She made sure they suffered." I sidestepped, "She may not have started all of this because of me, but every person she hurts now is on my shoulders." We were silent for a few moments, before I scoffed, "You know I've been avoiding Dina. Lily's told me to go see her several times, but I can't convince myself to face her. I don't even know why. She made it back safely. Griffin and Elsie are okay… But the way she jumped through that portal. It felt like she… blamed me. Blames me for all the bad shit that's happened to her…. She wouldn't be wrong if she did. The Red Queen tortured her to get to me. She was trapped in another world away from her husband and child for weeks because of me."

"My heart," Wyth forced me to look into his swirling eyes, "You have a capacity for guilt as large as your capacity for love. No one blames you, and if they do… Fuck em."

I snorted, "Caterpillar's rubbing off on you."

"I'm being serious, Alice. As a Queen there are times you have to make decisions that hurt the people around you. Anyone who loves you will understand the responsibility that is on your shoulders." He said.

I knew he was right, but I didn't feel that way. For nearly two years I'd been fighting for my family and friends, and it seemed like at every turn I only risked their lives more. "We'll talk about it more… later." I said, pressing a kiss to his cheek.

We continued to sweep the block, collecting anyone who came across our path. When the van was full, we sent Idalia back to the apartment, doubling back to ensure we didn't miss anyone. Just as were about to turn the corner, a shrill, "Maxton!" Pierced through the air.

"You've got to be f-fucking kidding me." He muttered, turning to face his mother and grandfather as they approached us. Dodo looked worse for the wear, his usually coiffed hair was slicked back as if he'd been nervously pushing it out of his face.

As soon as he got near us, he dropped to his knees, "Please, Miss Young, Maxton. The streets are no longer safe for anyone. I have no allegiance to the Queen of Hearts, I seek safety with you."

Claudia scoffed, "He is my son, father. He owes me for giving him life."

Whatever pity I'd had when I'd seen their disheveled appearances dried up the moment March's mother opened her mouth. "He owes you nothing." I snapped.

"Please ignore her, ma'am. My daughter is severely mentally disturbed-" Dodo began.

Claudia screamed, turning to kick her father in his supplicated position, "There is nothing wrong with my mind! Why do you never take my side." She reared back her leg to kick Dodo again, but Hatter grabbed her bicep, pulling her off balance. "How dare you touch me, you filthy fa-"

Before she could finish her insult I'd slammed my fist into her mouth, cutting off her words that she had begun to utter. Pleasure raced through me as I landed a second punch to her nose, "I can't tell you how much I've wanted to do that since I first met you."

"Maxton, how can you let them harm me. I. Am. Your. Mother." She spat blood at him, her brown eyes losing any sanity they may have held. "You couldn't even lay back right."

I had heard enough. Magick wrapped its way around my fist, responding to the rage I felt as she dared to use the abuse she'd forced March to endure against him. "You. Will. Never. Speak. To. My. Husband. That. Way.

Again." Every word I punctuated with another blow, her blood seeped onto the concrete. "No one else here may be able to stop you, but I've reached the end of my patience." My hair lifted as electricity built inside of me. My feet no longer touched the ground as I reached a hand out. Lightning cracked across the sky with a thunderclap, meeting my body as I floated above Claudia's bloodied body. I let the lightning flood through every molecule of my body, before I directed it straight into March's mother. Her single note scream met my ears, and I felt nothing but pride as she convulsed from the sheer power I'd sent into her. I lifted my other hand, another bolt of lightning responding to my magick. I turned raising my voice, feeling her magick respond to my call, "Rhosyn Black, I know you can hear me. I am the storm that you have conjured, and I am coming for you very, very soon." I released the bolt of magick I'd been holding, watching with satisfaction as it raced across the sky, leaving a silver scar behind. I had no doubt she had witnessed my message, but the rage and magick that had built inside of me was not satisfied.

I floated higher, lightning and thunder responding to me, racing through my body joining with my magick until I was overflowing with power. My skin burned, but I didn't care. I was nothing but my magick now. The Silver Queen had awoken, my only purpose was to restore peace to the worlds. I saw nothing but the sky as I moved higher, seeking my next target.

Strong arms wrapped around my midsection, and my power guttered out. My body went limp as I gasped from the sudden drain. I glanced down, finding Caterpillar's grey eyes brimming with fear. "Come back to me, princess."

"I'm here. I'm here. I'm here." I muttered, gripping his short hair as my body shook from the power intake.

He pulled me down onto the roof. The guys were all there, varying degrees of concern and fear on their faces. Wyth was on me the moment my feet touched the ground. "You cannot lose yourself to the magick that way. Never again."

"I-I I'm sorry." I choked out, glancing over the edge of the roof where I could see Claudia's body. Dodo was nowhere to be seen, I'm sure he had run as soon as he'd seen what Claudia had unleashed. "I killed her." My eyes filled with tears as I turned to March, "I should never have-"

"She deserved what she got." He stopped me, voice filled with darkness, "Claudia Danara was n-nothing but trash. She should have been executed years ago. Justice was served."

"He's right, sweetheart. She went too far. None of us are upset that you stopped her from hurting us ever again." Hatter added, "But I never want to see you fly away from us like that again."

"For the record though... Hot as fuck. All silver glowing, avenging angel. I've been rock hard since you started beating her ass." Cheshire said, "Naked, now. I think we all need to feel you, to know you're really... here."

I glanced to the other guys, but all of their eyes had turned to molten lava. I glanced up, finding the silver glowing scar still hanging in the sky. The energy that the magick had created in me still buzzed beneath the surface now that Caterpillar no longer held me. I needed my men to center me. I wasted no time stripping out of my clothes. To my surprise, Wyth was the first person before me, cock already hard and waiting. I fell to my knees, taking his length into my mouth. We moaned in tandem as he brushed the back of my throat. His fingers tangled into my hair, forcing me to take more of him until a tear ran down my cheek. My knees ached from the cool concrete, but as Cheshire appeared, naked, his lioness proudly inked on his chest every thought but pleasuring my men guttered from my mind.

He kneeled behind me, spreading my legs wide before teasing my swollen clit with his fingers, "Already so wet, just from sucking the King off. Are you ready for me?" I moaned, pressing back against his fingers. Ches groaned as his cock slowly stretched me, "Being inside you is the only thing

I think about day and night, Alice. You stepped into our world and became our sun, our perfect Queen. Don't ever forget that."

Wyth groaned as he slammed his cock down my throat, spilling his sweet seed across my tongue. No sooner than he had stepped away than March appeared, running a hand over my hair, before grabbing my chin. He ran the pad of his thumb over my tongue before replacing it with his cock. Unlike Wyth, he allowed me to set the pace. I sucked him in time with Cheshire's thrusts, teasing and sucking until March moaned and filled my mouth with his cum.

"Thank you, March." I said as he leaned down to kiss me.

"No, thank you. For always loving and protecting me." He whispered back, before allowing Caterpillar to take his place. Caterpillar stooped to my eye level, his hand wrapped firmly around my throat, while the other began to torture my nipples.

Cheshire groaned as my walls fluttered from Caterpillar's attention, and I felt his hot cum paint my insides. I moaned when he pulled away, leaving me aching and empty. Hatter was eager, hands gripping my hips within seconds of Cheshire leaving. But instead of sliding into my pussy, his fingers moved to my ass, stretching it. Caterpillar didn't give me a moment's peace, choking me as he explored every inch of my body except my pussy. When Hatter's cock began to invade my ass, I saw stars, "Please. Please. I... I need."

"Use your words, princess. Tell me exactly what you need." He teased, pinching my nipples hard.

"I need you." I keened as Hatter began to pound into me, "Inside me, I need you Roman, please."

"My perfect wife, already taken three loads for her husband's and still begging for more. Where do you want my cock, princess? Your mouth?"

I couldn't form words anymore, Hatter's relentless fucking of my ass had rendered me speechless. Caterpillar's fingers moved lower, lightly brushing over my clit, "Is this where you want me? Deep inside your pussy so you can cum all over two cocks?" I nodded, but instead of giving me what I wanted, he chuckled, "I think I want to try something new." His words stopped Hatter. He pulled out of me, and Caterpillar dragged me to my feet. My thighs were slick with cum, but I didn't care as Caterpillar led me to the edge of the roof, "Put your hands on the ledge. You will not move, is that understood?"

"Yes sir." I panted, the cool breeze did nothing for my heated skin.

He kicked my legs apart, "That's my good girl. Hatter is going to take your ass again, but Wyth and I are both going to fill this greedy little pussy."

My eyes widened at the idea. Wyth and Caterpillar were both large, nearly impossible to take one at a time, but the idea of both of them inside me at the same time was enthralling. Hatter slid back into my ass before I could prepare, causing me to yelp, my voice echoing over the city. Caterpillar lifted one of my legs, and I felt him begin to fill me. I kept my breathing steady, even as stars danced behind my eyes as both of my holes were filled to the brim. Once Caterpillar was fully seated, I felt fingers begin to stretch me beside his cock. The pain was delicious, sending shocks down my spine, but when Wyth's cock began to press in beside Caterpillar's I couldn't hold back my screams any longer.

"Look at you, so stuffed with us. Your pussy wants to be filled with your husband's, just relax." Caterpillar began to set the pace, all three of the men fucking me as I gripped the roof for my life. When fingers found my clit, rubbing in exactly the pattern that would send me over the edge, my body began to shake. Hatter was the first to finish, slamming into my ass with vigor with one final, echoing moan. I followed him to pleasure, an orgasm racing down my spine until I could feel nothing but the tidal waves of Caterpillar and Wyth as they both followed me to orgasm.

Caterpillar held me as I came down from the experience. I was sore in the best ways, but I was also completely drained. My magick slumbered as he helped me back into my clothes. Each of the men hugged and kissed me soundly, letting me know that I was loved before we left the roof.

I felt no guilt as we passed Claudia's body. She didn't deserve another moment of our time or attention. I squeezed March's hand, praying to the Creator that he would finally be free of his past.

Chapter 24

May 10th, 2159

Days had passed with no change to Wonderland's situation. New refugees arrived every day, but we made no progress on stopping the attacks or confronting Rhosyn. I was trying to distract myself, but as I approached Dina's apartment door, I couldn't find the courage to knock. I leaned against the wall, staring at the ceiling trying to get past the stupid feelings I had. This was my best friend, and I was terrified of her rejection. I wasn't the same girl I had been, and I wasn't sure that she could accept the woman and Queen I was today.

"You know most people knock." Griffin's voice startled me, and I turned to take him in. His red hair was longer than it had been at my wedding. He looked tired, but the bright smile he flashed me let me know he was okay.

"How is…"

"Don't ask me that. Just come inside and see for yourself." He opened the door, letting me enter first. Their apartment was painted in deep purples and decorated with soft velvety furniture. Elsie squealed when she saw me, running on her chubby legs to wrap around my calf.

I picked her up without hesitation, "You're getting to be so big." I cooed as she babbled half nonsensical words at me.

Dina appeared from the kitchen, an apron tied around her waist. "Alice! I didn't know you were coming to visit today."

"I'm sorry, I should have come sooner..." Guilt filled me at the genuine smile painted on her face.

"I'm going to take Elsie for her bath. Why don't the two of you sit down and talk?" Griffin said, taking his daughter from my arms. He had disappeared from the room before either of us could stop him.

Dina sat on the couch, and I awkwardly took the seat next to her. Neither of us broke the uncomfortable silence right away, but when it had lingered too long I said, "I'm glad you were able to get back safely."

"I'm sorry I abandoned you there. I know that's why you've been avoiding me. It was a real asshole move." Dina blurted out, "I assumed you and Duchess would follow right behind me."

Something about her words caused me to laugh, within seconds we were both giggling, our shoulders brushing. "You know I wasn't angry right? Things have just been so hectic, and I... I didn't want to face you, yet. All the horrible things that have happened in your life lately have been my fault."

She smacked my shoulder, "Shut up. You can't control what the Red Queen did any more than you can control that bitch dropping us into Undraland. None of that is your fault."

"You wouldn't be in danger if we weren't friends." I pointed out.

"When will you stop holding the weight of the world on your shoulders?" She joked.

I sighed, "I wish I could, but... I have a responsibility far larger than myself. To Wonderland. To Undraland. To all of the people and creatures that reside in both."

"That doesn't mean you need to take accountability for the actions of others. You aren't some evil Queen, torturing and killing indiscriminately. Even if you started to head down that road, I'd stop you, the guys would. You have a support system, Alice. Lean on us... Even when we make mistakes." Dina said.

I did have a support system of amazing people who eased the burden on my shoulders every day. Maybe that was the difference between me, Penthea, and Rhosyn. "Thank you, Di."

She wrapped her arms around me, her long black hair tickling my nose as we hugged. "You're my best friend, Ali. There's nothing you can do to get rid of me, even if we're in different worlds."

We chatted for a long time before Griffin joined us. For a few hours, I was able to pretend that we were in Griffin's apartment hiding away from the world before we were dealing with evil Queens and magickal problems. When my phone dinged I couldn't help the sigh that left me. It was time to return to reality.

> *Duchess: Can we go check the hospital? I want to know what happened to my mother.*

"I've got to go, but we'll do this again soon. I've missed you both." I stood, hugging both of my friends before heading out the door.

Duchess was waiting just outside the apartment building when I stepped outside. "Thanks for coming with me."

"None of us should go anywhere alone until we have dealt with Rhosyn." I responded.

To my surprise, Duchess flared with magick, a portal opening up. When I didn't immediately step through she said, "It's quicker. We can be back home in just a few minutes."

I shrugged, stepping through the portal. Short distances were less disorienting; by the time I'd recovered, Duchess stood next to me. We both stared at the half-destroyed hospital. It hadn't fully recovered from the first attack on it when we'd been sent to Undraland, but now it creaked with the blowing wind as if it might crumble completely at any moment. I glanced to Duchess, watching her face as she took in the destruction around us.

"Do you think that she is still alive?" I asked as we began to slowly pick through the debris around us.

"I don't know…" She trailed off, "I feel like I'd know it if I was an orphan."

I was slowly beginning to understand Duchess, with each new interaction we had the pieces of who she was became clearer. The snobby facade she always wore, the insecurity she hid, the abuse she had suffered. I was coming to appreciate the quiet strength she displayed by merely surviving in our world. We didn't speak as we searched the safe areas around the hospital.

"I don't think we're going to find anything out here." Duchess finally huffed after an hour of searching.

"It isn't safe to go into the building… If she was in there-"

"I know." She sighed, taking a seat on a large pile of rubble. "Not knowing is driving me crazy. As if she's lurking around any corner to snatch me away."

"Maybe Rhosyn took her in." I offered.

Duchess snorted, but before she could open her mouth a sudden pain in my head caused me to crumple to the ground. "I was never a fan of that woman for the record. She's just not stable." I rolled over, finding Penthea standing above me holding a long metal bar. My head throbbed from where she'd hit me with it.

Before she could land another blow, Duchess stood jumping in between us, "Mother. What the fuck?"

"I still can't believe my daughter has sided with you." Penthea addressed me, ignoring Duchess completely, "After you stole away my power and locked up her parents. Family really means nothing to anyone in my life. I guess she's more like my mother than I wanted to admit."

"Fuck you." Duchess snapped, "I'm not sorry that I wasn't the perfect magick wielding daughter you wanted. You were a horrible mother, I don't even know why I cared what happened to you."

Penthea finally moved her eyes to Duchess, "I did everything I could for you. Protecting you from the Queen of Hearts, trying to awaken the magick that should have lived in your veins. I gave you everything, and look at how you waste it."

I stood, gripping the throbbing pain in my head. I tried to reach for my magick, but I was too disoriented to use it. I glanced to Duchess, seeing the rage that was now written across her face. "You think you protected me?" She growled. "Do you know what I suffered when Rhosyn finally got her hands on me. What happened to Dad?"

Penthea went pale, she dropped the bar she was holding. "Vivica, where is your father?"

"Dead. The Queen of Hearts had had enough of her dud of a son. Once she confirmed that I was the legacy to her power, she slit his throat right in front of me. I'm surprised the two of you aren't best friends. You certainly took plenty of things from her playbook. The dark rooms, the beatings," Duchess was panting as she ranted. I held my breath as the reality of what she had been through at the hands of her mother and grandmother fully set in.

"Frederick is dead?" Penthea's voice was small, tears filling her red eyes. "No, she promised she wouldn't kill him so long as we cooperated with her plan."

"Well, she lied." Duchess scoffed, "I hope you enjoy your magickless, lonely existence, Mother. Because I hope I never see your horrid face again." She spat, turning to me. She summoned her magick, a portal appearing instantly, "Oh, and by the way. I have power and a family now." She said, before we both stepped through the portal.

We didn't speak until we'd stepped into the safety of our apartment building. "Are you okay?" She asked, grabbing my head and checking where I'd been hit.

"I'm fine, nothing March can't clean up easily. Are you okay?" I asked, searching her brown eyes.

"I don't know why I cared about finding her in the first place." She huffed.

"What you told her was true, ya know... You do have a family here." I said, wrapping her in a quick hug.

"Thanks, Alice." She said, sheepishly when I pulled away, "If you're good, I think I'm going to go shower."

I nodded, watching as she disappeared up the stairs. Once again, I was surprised by my cousin's willpower. I didn't know if I could withstand all of the betrayals and pain that she had.

Chapter 25

Caterpillar

May 12ᵗʰ, 2159

I stared down at Alice's slumbering features. Her dark brown lashes fluttered slightly from whatever dream she was having, her full lips begged me to kiss them soundly as they pouted slightly. It was nearly impossible for me to drag myself away from the goddess that I had married, who had saved me from a miserable life. But I had no choice. The citizens of Wonderland were at a tipping point. Being trapped in our building, packed together like sardines. Every day new refugees arrived, and every day the tensions rose. If we didn't find a larger, safer place to allow them to hide, we were going to have an angry mob on our hands. I didn't know of anywhere in Wonderland that could easily house nearly seven hundred people, but I had to try.

I closed the bedroom door quietly, allowing my wife to continue the peaceful sleep she deserved. As I entered the kitchen I was surprised to find Wyth there, sipping from a teacup as he investigated the cellphone I'd given him yesterday.

"Good morning," He greeted when he noticed me standing in the doorway, "There's more coffee on the stove if you'd like some. The tea here is far too weak for me."

I snorted. The Emerald King was so direct it was refreshing. I never had to guess what he was thinking, and I appreciated him for it. Hatter, March, and Cheshire were my brothers, men I had watched grow up, but my relationship with Wyth was something different. Not sexual by any means, not like what Hatter and March had, but I respected him, often sought him out when I needed to work through a problem that I didn't want to burden the others with. We didn't speak as I poured myself a cup of coffee, and slowly sipped it, staring at over Wonderland. District eleven and seven had been completely leveled. Hundreds of people were dead. I had no idea how we were going to ever rebuild Wonderland. I wasn't certain I even cared to. I could see the way Alice and Cheshire both itched to return to Undraland. I needed to talk to Hatter and March to feel out how they would feel about leaving Wonderland permanently once the business with the Queen of Hearts was complete.

Suddenly, the ground beneath my feet began to shake. Wyth grunted, "This isn't natural."

"It's Rhosyn." I growled, "She's trying to break past the wards."

As we rushed toward the front door, I heard the bedroom door slam open. Alice stepped out, already dressed, glowing lightly with her magick, rage painted across her face. "She's doing this because of me. I'll handle her. You need to protect the innocents."

"You're not going out there alone." I snapped.

"I'll go with her." Wyth said, "Go. Find the others, protect the innocents." I hesitated for a moment, but Alice didn't give me a choice as she pushed past me, rushing down the stairs toward the front door. "I'll protect her." He said with a quick squeeze of my shoulder.

I stood for a moment, watching after them, before heading down to our refugees. The room was in complete chaos when I entered. Henry stood atop one of the quotes, his magick heavy in the room, but people still shouted and panicked as the building shook around us, dust falling from the ceilings. Whatever magick he was working could not keep up with the sheer amount of fear that was taking over. Hatter spotted me first, "Is it the Queen of Hearts?"

I nodded, "Alice and Wyth are outside trying to handle it."

"We have to find a safer place for them, for ourselves." He insisted, "We've waited longer than we should have."

"We have nowhere to go. Most of the districts have been destroyed; the boonies are burning as we speak. Anywhere we go, she can find us." I hated feeling helpless and powerless when my people needed me.

Lily and Idalia approached, stopping Hatter's response. I could see the strain in Lily's pale skin from the shield withstanding damage. Her magick wouldn't hold out much longer. "We've got to start getting people out. Families and the elderly first." Idalia insisted.

"And take them where?" I snapped at her demanding tone. "Look at your wife. She can't continue to shield this building, much less protect anyone we try to move."

Idalia's brown eyes simmered with rage, but I could see the fear beneath as she looked over Lily. "We're sitting ducks if we don't do something."

A sharp whistle cut through the air, and we all turned to find March standing next to his father. "L-listen up. You came to us knowing that we would do anything to protect Wonderland. Nothing has ch-changed, I need all of you to give us time to come up with the best solution to keep you and your families safe." Magick was weaved into every word he spoke, strong enough that even I could feel it on my skin as it washed through the room. Instantly, I saw people relax, the room becoming quieter. Henry looked impressed as March climbed down, beelining to where we stood. "Hopefully that'll g-give us some time."

Hatter wrapped an arm around March, whispering something that made the man's cheeks turn a dusty pink. When the building shook again, I made a decision, "You have it under control down here. I'm going to see if I can help Alice and Wyth."

Hatter grabbed my arm, "We need you alive, bossman. I don't think we have time for your funeral rites."

"I have no intention of dying today," I said, gripping his arm with a promise.

As soon as I stepped out of the crowded room, Cheshire appeared at my side. He wore a simple outfit, but I could see the weapons hidden beneath the thin black cloth, "Let's go help our wife."

I nodded, taking the stairs two at a time. As soon as we stepped outside, we were swept into chaos. Alice and Rhosyn were at a standstill, silver and black magick flaring around them as they danced around the street. Wyth was locked in battle with three men who wore tattered red suits. Cheshire headed directly for him, pulling his favorite guns and popping off shots before anyone had noticed him arriving. His magick had grown in Undraland. His ability to be unseen was even more impressive.

I ran straight for Alice, watching in horror as the tiny Shadelume launched from her shoulder. The creature landed atop the Queen of Hearts bright red curls, causing the woman to shout and shake. It was almost comical, or at least it was until the tiny cat opened its mouth, revealing the tiny sharp fangs that lay there. I thought it was going to bite the Queen, but instead an indescribable sound left its throat. Rhosyn reacted instantly, her eyes rolling back as she dropped to her knees in pain. Alice rushed toward them, but the Queen recovered too quickly, ripping the creature from her head and tossing it through the air until it hit some nearby debris.

I saw Alice's indecision as she watched Nova hit the ground. "Watch out," I shouted, barely giving her a moment's notice as Rhosyn raised her glowing black hand, the ground shaking so hard I couldn't keep my feet.

"I've always hated the Shadelumes." Rhosyn said as she advanced on Alice, I could see the tracks of tears running down her face from whatever Nova had managed to do to her. Alice let her sword fall to her side, some words I could not hear left her lips before she ran to where her companion laid limp on the ground.

Rhosyn rounded on me, but hesitated as I rose to meet her, "Void," She snarled.

"Bitch." I growled back, "Too afraid to fight without your magick?"

I could see the rage in her eyes, how badly she wanted to attack me, but she stepped back, "Not today, Knight, but soon I'll be coming for your pretty little wife. You'd better hold her close, because when I'm done there won't be anything of her left."

I lunged forward, but Rhosyn portaled away before I could grab her. Instead, I stumbled, my arms closing around empty air. I recovered quickly, my eyes finding Alice first. She ran toward me, Nova's limp body laid across her arm as tears rolled down her face. "She has to be okay. She has to."

Cheshire appeared, hair tousled as he returned his gun to its holster. "Your mom can work her healing magick. Let's get inside before Rhosyn decides she wasn't finished."

I glanced around, the ground was littered with four bodies, all men who had chosen to support the Queen of Hearts. I didn't feel bad for them. They had chosen the wrong side, and death was all that awaited anyone who supported Rhosyn Black.

By the time I made it inside, Alcinda was already hovering her golden hands over the tiny Shadelume. The room was silent, everyone holding their breath as she worked her magick. When she stopped, Alice moved, running her hand over Nova's soft, white fur, "I've healed the broken bones and punctured lung from the impact, but her magick is... It's not replenishing as it should."

I saw a tear run down Alice's cheek, "She should not have been out there, shouldn't have been trying to help. She's just a baby."

"Let me try." Wyth said, brushing past me to lay his hands on Nova, "Maybe I can amplify her magick enough to..." He trailed off, a green glow wrapping around the tiny Shadelume as he worked his magick. When he stepped back, a tiny mewl filled the room.

Everyone breathed a sigh of relief as bright, glowing blue eyes blinked open. Alice scooped the creature into her arms, holding her close and whispering soft words. I glanced around the room, noticing the strain and stress painted on everyone's face.

"We can't stay here any longer," I announced, "If we can't find somewhere safe… It may be time to consider fleeing to Undraland."

No one spoke immediately, but a quiet cough from the door drew my attention. Sammy stood there, his greying hair slicked away from his face. When he met my eyes, he gave me a small nod. He stepped fully into the room, "Eumonia visited me alone not long before she died… She asked me to find a safe house. I don't know if she already knew what was coming, or if she just had good instincts… I guess it don't matter. Patrick and I have been working on an underground safe house in the suburbs. It's finally ready."

Eumonia had known. Maybe not that she would die, but she had known we would need somewhere safe to go. "We can't risk moving anyone through the streets." I pointed out.

Duchess stood, "Sammy can take me to the safehouse then I can open a portal. You all stay here, make sure everyone gets through before Lily drops the shield."

"I won't be able to protect the safehouse. It'll draw her attention." Lily pointed out.

"We won't be safe forever, but we might be safe long enough to put an end to all of this." Alice said.

With her words, everyone moved. Tonight we would get all of the refugees to safety. Tomorrow, we would formulate our final plan on ending Rhosyn's reign of terror.

Chapter 26

Alice

May 13th, 2159

I blinked against the harsh light that pierced the darkness I had been resting in. As my eyes adjusted, I found myself sitting in the garden at the castle in Undraland. Glancing around, my eyes landed on a blonde figure who was bent over smelling the pink roses that bloomed nearby. When she turned, my eyes filled with tears.

"Eumonia." I rushed toward her, throwing my arms around her without hesitation.

"Hello, Alice," I could hear the smile in her voice as she returned my hug, "The Creator is weak, our connection will not last long." She pulled away, hands resting on my shoulders as she searched my face for something.

"I'm so sorry you died for me." I felt the warmth of a tear running down my face, but I didn't care. Eumonia was the closest thing to a grandmother I'd ever had. While we may not have had much time together, what we did have was precious.

"Do not apologize, my sweet child. I lived far longer than anyone could dream of. Your life has just begun. I want you to live it." She pressed a kiss to my forehead, "Now, our time is very limited. The Creator weakens more and more each day. I've learned a lot at her side," Eumonia led me to a table motioning for me to take a seat, "I spent my final days desperately trying to

figure out how Rhosyn gained immortality. It isn't easy for a magick user to do. A feat of magick so intense it nearly destroys the body. I did it when I saved Wonderland, but Rhosyn is a mystery."

"Obviously, immortality doesn't mean she's invincible... Right?" I asked.

"Even in death I've found myself seeking answers. Thankfully, the Creator has gifted me an answer, and this opportunity to share my knowledge." Eumonia ignored my question, "When my grandmother was still the Queen of Undraland, Rhosyn was nearly forty years old. She had hidden herself away once she was old enough to understand who her grandfather was, but she didn't spend that time grieving his death. Like your grandfather, Oran, Rhosyn knew of curse magick. The Lyon's banned it, but that did not stop Rhosyn. She tapped into the very essence of Undraland, and she wove a dark curse."

"A curse?" I parroted, confused, "How can it be broken?"

"The curse she laid allows her access to all of Undraland magick. She is not truly immortal as I was, she feeds like a parasite from our home. If she can be cut off, if you can take away her power even for a moment, you can end her life."

"Why did she want my power?" Trying to fit the pieces of the puzzle together.

"Because you are special, Alice. The Creator blessed you with a power no magick user before you has held. You don't just strip away the magick of others; you absorb it, and it becomes a part of you. That is why, when you allow it, you can share that power with others. You are the biggest threat to Rhosyn, and she knows it." She explained, "With your heartmates and their magicks behind you, you are unstoppable. Capable of more than any Queen before you."

I sat in stunned silence for a long moment, trying to wrap my mind around what Eumonia had just revealed. Rhosyn wasn't immortal; I was powerful enough to stop her. Those words should have given me confidence, but instead it was more expectation, more responsibility. I had accepted that being the

Silver Queen meant I would never escape responsibility. To the people of Wonderland, to the entire world of Undraland, to my family, but most of all to myself. But killing Rhosyn? Ending a curse that had existed for hundreds of years? It seemed insurmountable.

"You are not alone, Alice Lyon, and you never will be." Eumonia said, her voice strained, "I can't stay any longer, but know that I will always watch over you."

"I love you," I shouted to the wind as she disappeared.

I awoke with a gasp, prompting Cheshire to sit up suddenly, "Are you okay?"

"A dream vision. Eumonia told me..." I shook my pounding head, trying to make sense of what I'd learned, "Rhosyn isn't immortal, we just need to cut her off from her magick."

"So, the plan hinges on Caterpillar?" He surmised, leaning back against the headboard.

"I don't know." I huffed, moving to rest my head on his naked chest. I ran my nails over the abs he'd recently started to develop, letting myself focus only on the beating of Cheshire's heart. A heart that had stopped once, not that long ago. I was desperate to find a way to protect my husbands. I glanced around the room. The bunker Sammy had brought us to was full of small rooms. I had claimed one for myself, and the guys had agreed that we would sleep in shifts. Cheshire and I had taken the room first, and as I glanced at the clock I realized we still had an hour left before

Hatter and March would arrive to switch off. I wasn't ready to discuss my dream with anyone else. I was in need of a distraction.

I sat up, pulling Hatter's shirt over my head and revealing my naked body. Cheshire inhaled deeply, his eyes filling with lust as I straddled his hips. I ran my fingers down his torso, brushing over his nipples eliciting a hiss from him. "Is my wife in need?" The blue of his eyes had disappeared, his lust causing his pupils to dilate.

"Make me forget." I said, before leaning down to press my lips to his. I squeaked when he grabbed my body, flipping us without breaking the kiss. I could feel his erection against my thigh as he began to kiss down my body, giving special attention to my nipples. I was already writhing with pleasure when he pushed my legs apart, burying his face between my legs until I was lifting my hips off the bed as an orgasm raced down to my curled toes. His tongue ring was still one of my favorite things. When I collapsed back down, panting, Cheshire didn't give me a moment to recover. He lifted me by my thighs, leaving only my head and neck resting on the bed as he teased my entrance with the head of his cock.

"So wet and ready for me, Ali." He murmured as he slowly pushed himself inside me. His grip moved to my lips as he bottomed out, filling me so completely at this angle that I could barely breathe. He set a rhythmic pace, rolling his hips so that he hit my G-spot with every stroke. When a second orgasm shuttered through me I couldn't stop the scream that left me. "Creator, your pussy feels so good fluttering around my cock, but I'm not done with you yet."

I panted as he pulled out, flipping me onto my stomach, "I need to feel all of your holes." He slapped my ass, before spreading my cheeks. I bit down on a pillow as his cock began to stretch my unprepared ass. "Such a good girl taking me like this. You love to be full of cock, don't you?" When I didn't answer immediately, he gripped my hair, pulling my head back, "Tell me how much you love this."

"I love the feeling of your cock inside of me, Cheshire. I love when you take my ass. I need you!" His hips slammed harder inside of me, but he didn't release his grip on my hair, "Ches, please."

"Please what wife?" He demanded.

"Please fill my ass with your cum." I begged. Cheshire let go of my hair, grabbing my hips and lifting them slightly as he pounded into my ass with abandon. When he groaned, I felt his hot cum paint my ass. He collapsed next to me, his chest rising and falling rapidly as he tried to catch his breath. "Thank you, husband," I said, pressing a kiss to his chest.

"Do you feel better?" He asked, pulling me into his arms.

I nodded, "Somewhat. I'm not sure how to handle the information Eumonia gave me, but it doesn't feel as overwhelming when I have you by my side."

"I'll do anything I can to help and protect you, Al. I don't have a reason to live except for you. All I need is for you to come out of this alive." He confessed.

"I'm not going anywhere." I promised, "We are going to get our happily ever after even if I have to turn into a monster to make it happen."

"You will never be a monster to us. Always our wife and our Queen." Cheshire said before kissing the top of my head. "Why don't we go take a shower before we have to tell everyone what you learned."

I nodded, allowing him to pull me into the small joined bathroom. It wasn't fancy or hardly large enough for two people, but we showered together, washing away the evidence of our time together.

Chapter 27

May 15th, 2159

"If you don't let me out of this bunker for a little while I'm going to go completely insane." Duchess snapped.

"It's too dangerous," Wyth argued, "I don't even want Alice out there, but she is the Queen."

I held in the snort that bubbled up. Wyth and Caterpillar had spent two hours trying to convince me not to go above ground, but I'd won. Not because I was Queen of anything, but because I'd threatened to withhold sex indefinitely if they didn't allow me to go investigate Rhosyn's current location. We'd been locked below ground for three days. No one had ventured into the city since we had fled our building. Hiding wasn't going to end this fight, and whether or not they wanted to admit it they knew I was right. "Duchess can escort me. The two of us alone can move in more secrecy than all of us together. I can put an illusion over us, and if we run into any danger she can portal us out." I said.

Caterpillar and Wyth both turned to glare at me, but Hatter spoke up, "There's no point in arguing with her." He stepped toward me, placing a hand on my cheek, "Be safe, sweetheart. None of us are worth a damn without you."

I leaned forward, kissing him, "We're just assessing our plan of attack. Nothing is going to happen."

Cheshire visibly cringed, "I wish you wouldn't say things like that."

I patted the sword strapped to my hip, then the daggers on my opposite side. Duchess had her twin axes strapped to her back. March pressed a pistol into my palm that I quickly tucked into the waistband of my jeans. "Anyone that fucks with us isn't going to make it out of the conflict alive."

Before we could leave, my mother appeared with Nova in her arms. "She told me I needed to come speak to you." I smiled, petting Nova's head. She was recovering nicely from her injury, but I wasn't willing to risk her life again. "You must be careful. Rhosyn is desperate, she wants all the power of Undraland and Wonderland combined. Killing you is the only way she can have that now."

My mother's words tickled something in my brain, and I turned reaching into my bag and producing the crown I'd claimed in the Tumtum tree in Undraland. "Let her come and try to take my crown."

I moved to place it on my head, but Wyth stopped me, "A Queen never crowns herself." The moment the crown sat atop my head, my magick buzzed with a wave of magick I'd only felt in Undraland.

"Let's go," I said, turning to Duchess. A portal appeared almost instantly, and I gave Duchess an impressed nod, "Your strength is growing."

Her face turned pink, but she said nothing as I stepped through the portal. I wasn't prepared for the downpour of rain I stepped into. My clothes were soaked through instantly, so I rushed underneath a nearby porch. Duchess stepped through the portal, cursing as she ran to join me. Her curls were plastered across her forehead, the mascara she'd been wearing ran down her face. I push the long strandards of my hair out of my face, and as we looked at each other we both burst out laughing

"We look like drowned rats," Duchess snorted, as she wiped away the black streaks on her face.

"Portal magick is not an exact science." I pointed out.

We stood there for a moment, staring out at the rain that showed no sign of letting up. Duchess sighed, "Should we just head back?"

I shook my head, "Maybe this will be a good cover. It's not likely anyone else is roaming around in the rain."

"I'm sure the state of our appearance will be enough to run anyone off anyway." She muttered, before we stepped back out into the rain.

"What exactly are you looking for?" Duchess asked after we'd been walking for well over thirty minutes. "She isn't going to just be standing out here waiting for you."

"I don't know exactly, but I feel... something." It was stupid and impossible to explain without sounding insane, but I could feel something calling out to me.

Duchess was silent for a moment, clearly mulling over what I had said. "What is it like? Your magick. I can tell that it's changed."

"Before we went to Undraland I felt in control of the magick. Mom trained me from the first moments my powers became apparent. As long as I slept enough and listened to it, I was the leader. Now... now it feels like the magick is alive inside of me, with its own wants." I explained.

"The rulers of Undraland are directly connected to its power," Duchess said casually.

I stopped, "How do you know that?"

"Edik spent a lot of time droning on and on about the history of magick." She responded.

My mind raced. If I were directly connected to the power of Undraland, Rhosyn couldn't take the throne while I lived. Even with her curse, she was powerless in that world without a crown atop her head. It was a genius failsafe, only something the Creator could have implemented. I opened my mouth to tell Duchess what I'd just figured out, but a woman's scream echoed around us. We both stiffened, glancing around for any sign of where it had come from. When a second scream followed we both ran in the direction of the sound. I slid to a halt as we turned the corner. Standing in the center of the town square was Rhosyn and Penthea. I noticed Eumonia's statue was destroyed, her giant stone head laying several feet away. Rage bubbled up in me at the sight, but I stayed rooted to the spot. Rhosyn backhanded Penthea, causing her to fall to the ground, "You were always useless. To my plan, to my son, and most of all in producing in my heir."

"I did everything I could to bring her magick forward." Penthea spat, as she returned to her feet. "Why didn't you tell me about Eumonia, Oran, and Alcinda? How could I compete with a line blessed by our fucking Creator?"

Rhosyn dealt another vicious blow, "I'm sick and tired of your excuses."

Duchess moved, her twin axes in hand, one of them already swinging down toward Rhosyn before I could move. Rhosyn turned with just enough time to duck under her swing, delivering a blow to her stomach that caused Duchess to double over with a shout. I grabbed the vorporal sword, rushing in without hesitation. When Rhosyn laid her eyes on me she snarled, taking in the silver crown atop my head, "I'll take your head before I allow you to taunt me with a crown that should belong to me."

"Go ahead and try." I growled, bending my knees and swinging my sword slightly. The rain dulled its magickal glow, but it still cast light over Rhosyn's pale face. It was then that I noticed her dark eyes weren't on me. Duchess was standing to my left, soaked with rain, but on her feet. Rage was painted across her features in a way I'd never seen before.

"You killed my father." She said, her voice monotone and unfeeling, "I may not kill you today, but I'm going to damn well try." She launched herself at Rhosyn, axes swinging faster than my eyes could track. Rhosyn hissed as Duchess cut a line down her chest, red blood blooming across her skin. When I moved to assist, Duchess barked, "This is my fight."

I knew she couldn't kill Rhosyn so long as she had her magick, but I understood that this was personal for Duchess, so I lowered my sword. I watched as they fought, dancing around and exchanging blows as if the rain didn't beat down on us. After a particular harsh blow, Duchess sagged, dropping to her knees as blood dripped from the edge of her mouth.

Rhosyn gripped her hair, "You are nothing but a disappointment to the great Red King's lineage. I should have killed you as a child when you showed no talent."

Rhosyn raised her hand, and I moved, but before I could stop her Penthea appeared. A giant rock in her hand that she slammed down on Rhosyn's head, "That is *my* daughter. She is *my* legacy." My aunt's scream echoed. Rhosyn turned on her, and before anyone could react Penthea's head rolled off her shoulders, hitting the ground with a wet thud.

Duchess screamed tears rolling down her face. I made it to her side, grabbed her midsection to stop her from attacking Rhosyn again. "This is over. You'll face me. Here. Tomorrow at noon. We will end this. You want my crown, we'll see if you can take it."

Rhosyn cackled, "Tomorrow at noon then." She glanced down at Penthea's beheaded body, "At least I took the trash out for you." With those words she disappeared in a flurry of black.

Duchess rushed to her mother's decapitated body. Sounds of pain leaving her throat as she carefully picked up her head, gently bringing it back to her mother's body. I sat beside her, resting my hand on her back. "She saved my life." Duchess whispered, "After everything she did to me... I don't understand."

"People are complicated, Vivica. Penthea suffered in her childhood, she was an outsider in her family. People feared her long before she became the Red Queen. I don't think she understood love, but... she was still your mother." I said, trying to comfort her.

"We need to bury her." She responded, standing.

And so we did. We found some soft ground nearby and dug with our hands until the hole was deep enough to hold Penthea's body. We carefully lowered my aunt into her makeshift grave before returning the dirt over her. It wasn't a beautiful ceremony, but we both had tears running down our faces when we stepped away covered in mud and soaked from the rain. "Tomorrow I will kill Rhosyn Black, and we will begin a new, more peaceful world." I promised.

"I know." Duchess said, a portal appearing behind her with ease, "Thank you for caring."

"We're family. No matter what, I'll always be here for you." I said, before stepping through the portal and back into the bunker.

Caterpillar rushed toward me when he saw the state of me, "What happened?" He demanded as Duchess stepped through the portal.

"We found Rhosyn... Tomorrow at noon we're putting an end to this war." I declared to the room, meeting eyes of all of my family and friends. "Penthea Rose sacrificed her life for her daughter today. No one else will die for Wonderland. Is that understood?"

A chorus of agreement moved through the room. Duchess inclined her head, before disappearing to her room. "What happened?" Hatter asked, following me as I headed to our room.

"It's not my story to tell." I waved him off, before stopping, "Thank you. For convincing me to stand by Duchess when they found her. I'm glad she has you as a friend."

He smiled, his green eyes twinkling, "I adore you, Alice Evageline Lyon. There is not a day that goes by that you don't warm my heart. I knew Duchess just needed people who could show her what love is. If anyone knows, it's you."

I leaned up, kissing him, "Hayden O'Hare you are one mad man. In the very best of ways."

His laughter followed me into the shower, breaking through the fear and sadness that had filled my heart. Tomorrow was going to be the first day of a life of freedom for me and my husbands. I could not fail.

Chapter 28

May 16th, 2159

We didn't sit around discussing a plan. We'd spent our night huddled together, stolen time for five hearts that now beat as one. As we approached the center of town I took a moment to look at my men. Caterpillar stood to my right, a tight black t-shirt and simple black cargo pants were all he wore aside from his boots. No weapons were visible on his person, but I had no doubt he was the most armed of us all. His hair was the longest I'd ever seen it, the top reaching his brow. He spoke quietly to Cheshire on his right. Cheshire would push his magick to its limit today. I couldn't work any illusion spells today, so he would stretch his invisibility over himself and Caterpillar any moment. Something they had apparently been working on in secret for months. Caterpillar had found some kind of control over his void power, he'd hidden this information from everyone until he'd tested it. Cheshire's face was pale. I could see his nerves in the lines of his muscles beneath the purple shirt he wore. Something about its color brought a smile to my face. Even now, when everything could change, he held onto who he was. I admired that about him. My eyes turned to Wyth on my left. His wore his armor today, only his helmet remained at the bunker. His swirling eyes met mine, a glimmer of fear in their depths. Our love story had only just begun, and the chances of it being cut short by the Queen of Hearts hung over us. He leaned down, capturing my lips with his. I wrapped my arms around his neck and allowed him to hold me for just a moment, my feet dangling just above the ground. I felt his power intermingle with mine. When I dropped to the ground, silver glowed beneath my skin, while green fire burned in his eyes. I could feel his power twisting inside of me, boosting me unlike anything I'd ever felt before.

I turned to Hatter, seeing his disgruntled face, "Staying back here with March is not a punishment. If any of us are hurt, you two are the final line of defense." I said, reaching to snatch the black beanie he wore off his head, putting it over my hair, "For good luck." He pulled me into his arms, squeezing me tightly while pressing a kiss atop my head. I had left my crown behind with Duchess. If I died, my mother or Lily could take my place as Queen of Undraland. They should have been in line to the throne before me.

"You don't need luck, Ali. You're g-going to end that bitch today." March's words were filled with his magick, punching through my body like a command. Not a prophecy, but his demand of me. I pulled him into our hug, sandwiched between their warm bodies settled any nerves I had. Our journey had not been easy, and so it would not end today. No matter what Rhosyn believed.

I stepped away, turning to look at them all one last time, "I want you all to know... There has not been a moment since Hatter saved me from the Hearts Club that I regret. Whatever road we have walked together, I would not want to walk it with anyone else. Once this is over, we are done putting the citizens of Wonderland or the Creator's whims before us. We may rule, but only on our terms."

"We all love you, princess. We don't need a speech because you're going to walk out of this alive." Caterpillar said, before Cheshire laid a hand on his shoulder. Cheshire would drain his magick quickly if we didn't move, so I let Wyth grab my hand. With one last look at Hatter and March, I let myself be pulled toward the town square.

Rhosyn was waiting when we arrived. The Jabberwock chained to a building nearby, saliva leaking from its mouth as its white eyes took us in. Wyth stared it down, something primal overtaking him. A hunter's mask over his face, he moved away from me as I approached Rhosyn, refusing to acknowledge her as he kept his eyes trained on the beast.

"Only the two of you? Did your husbands finally decide you weren't worth risking their lives for?" She mocked. As I stared at her, I really saw her for the first time. Her skin was translucent, blue veins showing beneath. There was nothing but blackness in her eyes, as if any emotion she'd once held had been stripped away from her. The wound Duchess dealt her yesterday still festered across her chest as if she'd refused to even clean it. She was soulless, I could feel her poisoned ambition as she moved toward me. The curse she'd cast hadn't just hurt Undraland, it had sapped the life from her. Only magick kept her alive now, and I was her great equalizer. "Nothing to say? Pity to go to your death in silence."

"Why would I waste my breath on you?" I said, before magick flared out from me. Green and silver striking her in the chest. The ground shook under my feet, but I didn't let it throw me off balance. The Vorporal sword was in my hand in a second. I ran at her, but she was prepared for me, ducking under the arc of my sword as she pulled a dagger from nowhere, aiming for my leg. I pivoted, catching her wrist before she could deal a blow. She shoved away from me, black magick curling around her aiming for me. When it hit my shoulder, the golden shield Lily had laid over my skin before we left flared to life. It couldn't stop her physical blows, but I was immune to her magick for now.

She let out a frustrated shriek, a flurry of magick and blades came at me. A blade sliced along my cheek. The cut stung, but I shook the pain away. Raising my left hand to the sky, thunder rumbled over head, lightning arc down around me. Electricity caging Rhosyn and I in a small space. I hit her with three blasts, watching with little interest as she collapsed to the ground, her body shaking from the electricity pumping through her veins.

I took the moment to find Wyth. He stood atop the building, feet away from the Jabberwock. A greatsword was in his left hand while his right was flared with his green magick. The Jabberwock thrashed in its chains, that was when I noticed the muzzle locked around its jaw. Rhosyn didn't have control of the beast at all; she was starving it for her own gain. I reached for his magick, pulling on it gently until he turned to look at me. I pointed to the muzzle, trying to communicate what I could. The Jabberwock was just a beast, and beasts could be tamed.

"You think a few little zaps could stop me." Rhosyn hissed as she stood.

Her puffy red dress was smoking in an almost comical way, but I just shrugged, "It was worth a try."

She raised her arms, and I had to dive away as a portal opened up where I'd been standing. She chased me, opening swirling portals on all sides of me, but I managed to stay one step ahead. A roar drew her attention away. Wyth was now mounted on the Jabberwock's neck, its muzzle cut into pieces on the ground. The beast flared its violet wings wide, taking flight with an ear piercing screech. Wyth flew the creature around for a moment, as Rhosyn gaped up at the sky. When it dove down, it's maw agape with white lightning she wasn't prepared. A blast hit her side, and she yelled as her right arm blistered and burned. Her black magick faded for a moment, and I ran trying to reach her before she could recover. Just as I reached her, she whirled toward, a dagger in her uninjured hand. She plunged it into my hip, burning pain rushing down my leg and lower stomach. I gripped the blade, ripping it from where it was embedded and throwing it away from us. A laugh ripped from her throat, and I couldn't stop my fist as it smashed into her face. She coughed on the blood that began to fill her mouth as I stumbled backward. Unable to ignore the pain of the knife wound.

"I have not plotted for centuries for you to ruin it here today." She hissed, as she stood. Before she could take step, a haunting sound came from our left. March stood alone, his mouth open, arms raised. I furrowed my brows, the magick was weak, nothing like what I'd felt from him recently.

The Queen of Hearts threw her head back and laughed, "The weak boy? That is who you think can defeat me?"

"No, but my wife can." Hatter said from my left. White magick flared as he laid both of his hands on my hips. I felt the knife wound instantly heal itself under his warm hands.

"Our wife." Cheshire corrected as he appeared behind Rhosyn. His skin was slightly paler than usual, but the gun in his hand fired twice before I could think about it. Rhosyn screamed as the bullets ripped through both of her kneecaps.

"Princess, it's time." Caterpillar said from beside me. We moved as a unit, Wyth's green magick flared behind us as Caterpillar grabbed Rhosyn's shoulders. My own magick responded, swirling to life inside me, an ancient response.

She thrashed and screamed viciously as every ounce of magick was drained from her under his touch. My silver magick flared bright, and I pressed a hand to her chest, "No more stolen magick. No more deaths. No. More. Rhosyn." I whispered into her ear as I found the empty well of her magick burned deep in her core. I gripped it, raising the vorporal sword, "The Queen of Hearts reign ends today."

I ripped the well of her magick from her body, siphoning every piece deep into my own well. The vorporal sword cut through her neck like butter once I'd ensured no magick remained within her. Her headless body slumped forward when Caterpillar dropped it. Unfortunately the magick he'd been holding back folded directly into me in an instant. Black overtaking the silver of my magick inside of me.

Wyth caught me as I pitched backwards, my body shaking from the power influx. "I can take it back." Caterpillar shouted as he ran to my side.

"She won't be able to adjust to it if you do that. The magick must go somewhere." He responded. All of the guys kneeled around me. I could do nothing but stare at the grey sky as my body seized. I willed my magick to respond, to fight back against the power influx, but nothing I tried worked.

A tear rolled down my cheek from the pain. Wyth voice broke through the pain, "We are her heartmates. We should be able to do something." I could hear the panic in his voice, but it sounded muffled, far away.

I felt hands on my body, warm and large. Colors danced in my vision, green, white, purple, indigo. And in the center, silver twisted with black, but slowly. Ever so slowly. The silver glittered brighter, reaching for the other colors. Some of the pain eased, my hearing returned. I blinked and found myself staring up at my husband's worried faces. My skin was tight and my muscles ached, but I had control again.

"You're okay?" March whispered, his hand squeezing mine.

"I'm okay." I whispered back, stroking the side of face. I sat up, noticing the blood that puddled around us. "It's over?"

"Rhosyn Black has joined the Red King in death." Wyth confirmed, "We did it. Together."

We all sat there for a moment, staring around what had once been the city center. At the already decaying body of a woman we'd just killed together, a woman who had been torturing us and the citizens of Wonderland for years. It didn't feel real, but as I stood I could feel a sense of peace in my gut that hadn't been there before. "Let's go tell the others. The citizens of Wonderland should celebrate tonight."

"And tomorrow?" Caterpillar asked.

"We have time to figure that out." I said, allowing him to sweep me into his arms.

"Yes we do." He smiled, and began walking back to our temporary home.

Chapter 29

May 20th, 2159

My body still ached, and I had spent most of the last four days sleeping, but the happiness that filled the bunker was infectious. My mother had taken the lead on explaining to the citizens of Wonderland about the home world of the magick users. While some people were hesitant the majority of people wanted a build a new life. Lily, Idalia, Mom, Rab, and Duchess had taken the time to speak with everyone in the bunker, explaining every detail they could about Undraland, and how different life would be there. I appreciated the break the guys and I had been given to recover. I was not at full power, and it would likely take months for me to recover.

"I'm ready to open the portal and allow people to move through." Duchess announced as we ate lunch together, "I was just giving you time to rest before we go."

I glanced to Wyth and Cheshire who both gave me enthuasitic nods, "I think we're ready, Viv. Wonderland is beyond repair. There's an entire world waiting for us to rebuild it."

"We should go above ground to do it. Wyth wants to test out the motorcycles in Undraland." Caterpillar said.

"How quickly can everyone be ready?" I asked.

"They already are." Mom finally piped in, "Henry has all the magick users organized to make this run as smoothly as possible. Wyth is going to take the Jabberwock through first, release it into its natural habitat so it doesn't attack anyone."

I nodded, "Sounds like a good plan. Give me two hours and I'll be ready." I was eager to return to Undraland. I wanted to see it now that the curse was broken.

A thousand people stood on the street, staring at the large, swirling black portal that Duchess had produced. I starred up at the shimmering golden dome, imagining how Eumonia would feel knowing that we were finally returning her people to their home.

Henry and Joshua stood side by side, helping people through the portal slowly. Henry eased the fear of the magick users, while Joshua guided the regular humans through. It was odd to see them together, something about seeing March and Hatter's dads alive and working together to support us was unimaginable. I hoped they continue to do so for their communities once we were settled in.

Rab approached me, "Everyone is doing well. Your mother runs a tight ship."

"She sure does." I snorted.

We fell into a comfortable silence for several minutes, before Rab cleared his throat. "I know... I'm so glad you and Caterpillar share so much love." I turned to look at him, taking in the pink of his cheeks I nearly choked.

"You are going to ask me if its okay if you marry my mother, aren't you?" I said.

His blue grey eyes widened, and then he laughed, "You are far too much like her. I guess the Ainsworth men just can't resist a Lyon woman."

"As long as she says yes and is happy, I'm happy, Jonah. You both deserve to find love again after all that you've been through." I said as I patted his arm.

"I can never replace Mary Anne and she can never replace Charles, but it is good to be seen… and loved by someone." Rab responded, before pulling me into a hug.

"I'm happy for you both." I assured him.

He opened his mouth to say something, but someone shouted, "Alice, we need you over here. Now!"

I turned, running to find Duchess on her knees. The portal seemed to flicker slightly. I skidded to a halt, "You're burning out."

"No," She panted, "I can do this."

"You might kill yourself." I tried to reason with her, "We can stop. Wyth is there, he and the Knights can care for the people who have already gone through."

"No." She said more sternly, "It'll take me weeks to recover, you know that. We'll be trapped here. I have to do this today. It's worth risking."

"Not your life, Vivica." Hatter snapped at her, "I can't let you kill yourself."

"She won't." I interrupted. I glanced back up at the golden shimmering dome, "She'll use me. I can filter the magick in the shield to her, power her up. Everyone will have to move fast, but we can do it."

"You're barely recovered. Absolutely not." Hatter said.

"It's the only way. You have to move people through." Before he could say another word, I levitated, letting electricity rush through my body. "Duchess, grab my ankle, reach toward my magick. Take what you need."

She followed my instructions, and I felt the drain on my power begin instantly. My eyes widened as I felt the sheer amount of power she was using for a portal of this size. She would have died before everyone could get through. I lifted my arms, reaching for the magick of the dome. It responded eagerly, flooding into me like it was coming home. My skin heated uncomfortably as gold and silver swirled in my chest, before siphoning to Duchess. I closed my eyes, feeling the magick instead of seeing it. I spiraled deeper into the power, yanking harder, forcing my well of power to grow to accommodate every ounce of magick that Eumonia had placed into the barrier. It burned, but I pushed through. Eumonia's power and mine would save the people of Wonderland one last time.

Hours passed in minutes, and I lived in the realm between pain and ecstasy. I was power as I absorbed and siphoned all of the magick in the dome. Hundreds of years of reinforcement flooded my veins. When the burn of my skin became unbearable I opened my eyes, only to be blinded by the silver light that surrounded me. I glanced down, seeing about two hundred heads moving below me. Duchess' grip on my ankle didn't waiver, but my magick was stretched thin. I groaned as she began to pull from my own reserves, the dome's magick already depleted.

"I can't." My throat was raw as I collapsed to the ground. Duchess moved her hand to my shoulder, "I'll finish it. Maybe..."

"No." March stepped forward. He knelt before me, "T-take mine." He held out his hand, slender fingers steady as he grabbed my hand, "Use my magick to get us all home."

"You won't have anything left." I shook my head.

"I don't need magick, Ali. I only need you." March insisted, "So long as you're alive and healthy, you are all the magick I could ever want in the world."

"Maxton?" Henry's voice sounded behind us, "Are you sure?"

He looked to his father, "This is the greatest thing my magick will ever accomplish."

Henry nodded, clapping him on the shoulder, "I'm proud of you, son. You will make a great King."

March turned back to me, holding out his hand again. I stared into his warm brown eyes, searching them for fear or hesitation. When I found nothing but love and determination, I clasped his hand. I gently prodded the spot in his mind that held his power. He threw open the doors for me, handing over every ounce of his magick to me without hesitation. I breathed it in, tasting honey on my tongue as I siphoned the power through my well, and directly to Duchess. The three of us stood like that until Hatter's voice broke through the trance, "It's time to go."

He lifted me into his arms, while March helped Duchess to her feet. Together we faced the swirling black portal as it began to shrink. As we pushed through the darkness I squinted the two suns of Undraland shining down on us as we appeared just outside the castle door.

As soon as the portal closed, Duchess dropped to her knees. Edik appeared from nowhere, rushing to her side, "Ledger has an infirmary already set up. Cheshire told us what to expect."

"Did everyone make it through safely?" I asked, ignoring the pain in my throat and body.

He nodded, "You saved everyone, my Queen."

"Thank the Creator." I murmured before I black out.

Chapter 30

Six Months Later

November 28ᵗʰ, 2159

"Is it ever going to go away? The citizens look like they may start bowing to me every time I walk into a room." I complained as I sat in a hot bath, scrubbing over my glowing silver skin.

Wyth laughed, "Everyone should bow when you enter a room, my heart. You are the Queen of Undraland."

"Semantics." I rolled my eyes, standing from the tub, "Why don't you show me how a queen should be worshipped?"

He grinned as he pulled my hips toward his face, sucking my already pounding clitoris into his mouth. I moaned as he devoured me, bringing me to a heart stopping orgasm in minutes. "I like the glow, my heart. Stop complaining about it."

I laughed, as I moved down his body, finding his hard cock and slowly sinking down his length. I set the pace, moving my hips in taunting circles, watching his face as he held himself back. His beautiful umber skin called for my nails, and I couldn't stop myself from scratching down his chest, watching the dark lines appear with satisfaction. "You are mine, Emerald King."

"And you are mine, Silver Queen." He murmured before pulling me down to kiss me soundly. He grabbed my hips, setting a faster pace until he was spilling himself inside me. We laid there for a moment before he chuckled, "We need to actually get ready for this dinner, you know."

"Shit, I knew I was forgetting something." I stood, climbing back into the tub to rinse off quickly.

We didn't have as many family dinners now that everyone was busy with turning Undraland into a suitable home for the magick users and humans alike. I put on a simple blue gown that had appeared in my closet yesterday. The castle now made its power known, ensuring all of its residents had our needs and wants met. While some of the Undralandian population had awoken after the curse was broken, many of them were suffering from severe trauma, and were struggling to adjust to waking up over a hundred and fifty years after they been cursed to stone. Joshua and Henry had formed a team to assist each of them with finding a path in life that would be healing for them.

As I stepped out the room, Sheridan came up to my side, "Queen Alice, Duchess has requested a private meeting next week and Sporekin and the young ones are insisting on returning to the Tumtum tree to try and heal it."

I sighed, "I think it's time to allow them to return to their home, Wyth has ensured the Jabberwock remains on its mountain."

"I'll pass that along. Is there anything you need before I take off for the night?" She asked. I smiled at the blue haired girl. She had shown up at the castle three months ago insisting that we needed her help to run our kingdom. She'd been right, having her to field issues and complaints allowed me far more time with my men. I'd even had time to start working on adapting Earth recipes to Undralandian food. So far everything I'd made had been approved by both Nova and Cheshire. Those two had become thick as thieves when the small Shadelume had finally gained her voice last month.

"Enjoy your night off, Sheri." I hugged her before shooing her away.

I threw open the dining room doors, finding everyone already seated and waiting for me. Wyth wore a smug expression. I still couldn't figure out all of the hidden hallways in the castle, and he took great pleasure in beating me to meetings any chance he could.

My mom, Rab, Lily, Idalia, Lewis, Henry, Joshua, and all of the guys grinned as I took a seat. We started to dig in instantly, banter and joke flying across the table. Griffin, Dina, and Elsie were touring home this evening, because they refused to continue to stay in the castle, citing strange noises in the night, but I knew that they had been trying for another baby over the last few months and wanted to raise their children in a normal home. I was happy for my family and friends as they found love and joy in their lives for the first time.

I collapsed back onto the bed, my skin slicked with sweat as Hatter and March finally finished. "Tonight was nice. We really should do family dinners more often."

Caterpillar grunted, "It's gross watching Rab fawn over your mother. I know they're newly married, but..." He gave a fake shiver, "They're old."

"Technically you're old too." Cheshire pointed out, causing me to snort.

"Wyth is way older than me." Caterpillar shot back.

"Woah, what did I do to be dragged into this?" Wyth responded as he tossed me one of my night gowns. "I was frozen at thirty-one. So technically, you are still the oldest of us."

"Owned." Cheshire belly laughed. Caterpillar kicked him off the bed, but that didn't stop the laughter for a moment.

"What do you think Duchess wants to talk to me about privately?" I mused. I'd been thinking on it all night. She'd refused to come to dinner, and now we were planning to meet privately tomorrow.

"Maybe she's finally going to accept her official place in the kingdom." March offered up, "S-she's been refusing to take the title of Princess, even though it would rightfully be hers. Lily and Idalia love being princesses." Idalia and Lily were focused on raising Caroline to honor Ilaria, granting them titles within our kingdom had felt like the least we could do after everything they had been through.

I shook my head, "I doubt it. I can't even get her to accept a royal stipend for being the only portal magick user."

"Maybe she's pregnant." Cheshire offered up from the floor. We were all silent for a moment, before I burst into laughter.

"She glares at any man that approaches her that isn't Edik or Kori." I pointed out.

"My Knight's would never impregnant a member of the royal family without a marriage contract in place." Wyth insisted.

I shrugged, "I guess I'll find out tomorrow."

We all curled up, and I drifted to sleep surrounded by the warm bodies of the men I loved.

I stood in the center of my flower field. It bloomed in bright blues and purples, and I bent down to pick one of the flowers. When I turned, each of my husbands stood behind me, dressed in matching suits of silver. I glanced

down, finding that I wore a silver gown as well, cut to perfectly show off my body.

"Welcome my chosen," The Creator's voice filled the meadow. "I am sorry I have been silent these last few months. It took time for me to regain my strength."

"Is everything okay?" I asked, finding her blue figure of light standing nearby.

"All is well, Alice. You have fulfilled your destiny. Undraland is healing, more magick returns each day. There is finally peace in the realms." She said, easing the anxiety in my chest, "I have come today with gifts." She approached, "First, I know that the marriage customs of Earth are the ones you follow. I want to present you rings for you and your final heartmate."

A thin silver band encrusted with tiny glowing stones appeared in the center of my palm. I gasped as I took in its beauty, "This is beautiful."

"You have long since said the vows of your love, so I do not feel the need to officiate a ceremony, but," Each of the men suddenly had a ring that matched mine in his palm, "In the eyes of your Creator, the five of you share a bond so strong it will ascend the planes of life and death. So long as one of you lives, so shall the others." She turned to me, "And my final gift. A gift of knowledge." The Creator laid hands on my cheeks, "For the sacrifices you have made and the power you hold, you have been granted immortality. You shall rule over Undraland so long as you wish. Should you have an heir, you may retire from the crown, but only you will ever be my chosen champion."

"I'm immortal?" It was impossible to wrap my mind around, even as I stared at the glowing figure of the Creator.

"You and your heartmates will walk the wilds of Undraland until the final star has died." She confirmed, "You will know a life full of love and joy."

"I... Thank you." I said, unsure what other words to say.

"No, Alice Lyon, thank you. You have sacrificed much for the worlds my sister and I created. A long and happy life is the least that you deserve." She *said, pressing a kiss to my brow, "I am always with you, but I hope never to call on you again."*

With those words, the Creator disappeared, leaving me and my men alone in this dream world. I glanced at the flowers, and for just a moment I was transported to the first moment my father brought me here. Every moment I spent in this field played through my mind. A few tears ran down my face, before I stepped into the waiting arms of my husbands. We had an eternity ahead of us, and I truly could not wait to begin our lives together.

Epilogue

Duchess

November 30th, 2159

I paced outside of Alice's office, unable to enter the room. I shouldn't have been nervous. There was no reason to believe she would deny my request, but... "Come in, Viv." Alice's voice cut through my thoughts. I sighed, opening the door.

Alice sat in a plush leather chair; her long blonde hair pulled back into a ponytail. While her skin held a permanent silver glow, she didn't look like a Queen dressed in tight jeans and a simple white shirt. I wasn't jealous of her the way I had been at one point in time, but the happiness she had with her husbands... I wanted that. I wanted to finally be happy. "What can I do for you?"

"I want to leave Undraland." I blurted out.

Her crystal blue eyes widened, "Are you not happy here? Has someone done something? I will-"

"No... Everything here is perfect. I just... I just want some time to discover who I am. To see the world and find my place within it." I admitted.

"Oh." She sat back in her chair, studying my face with intense curiosity. "Will you pop in and let us know you're okay occasionally?"

I nodded, my heart pounding in my chest, "I'll visit at least once a month."

"I don't want you to feel trapped here, Duchess. I just want you to know that we all care for you. You'll always have a home with us." She responded seriously. "And I'd prefer you didn't go alone. There is still a lot of danger in this world."

I deflated, "I don't know..."

Alice stopped me, "Give me a couple of hours, get your bags ready. If you don't like my solution, then you can just do whatever you have in mind. Deal?"

"Deal." I said, rushing from the room to pack my bags. I was truly excited for the chance to have complete freedom for the first time in my life.

I stood at the doors of the castle, tapping my foot impatiently. When Alice and Wyth appeared, I breathed a sigh of relief, but I stiffened when Edik, Kori, and Ledger appeared behind them bags strapped to their backs. "They are your solution?" I hissed, "I don't need guards."

"I agree." Ledger muttered, and I rolled my eyes. I still couldn't figure out why the man hated me so much, but at this point I didn't care. I just wanted to leave the castle.

"They aren't guards or even escorts." Wyth said, "Imagine them as your tour guides. These men know every inch of Undraland like the back of their hands. No matter where you end up, they can ensure your safety."

"And if I want to explore Earth?" I asked, placing a hand on my hip. "What will they do then?"

"We will keep you safe and enjoy exploring with you." Edik said, "I promise we have no intention of getting in your way. You can lead us wherever you'd like to go. I only ask that if we run into anyone in need, you allow us to assist."

"I'm not a heartless monster," I snapped, and then sighed. "Is this the only way you're not going to freak out?" I asked Alice.

She winked, "You got it. You are important to me and to this world. We can't allow you to go off alone without any protection."

"Fine, but one of you is carrying my stuff." I gave in, "And we're starting in Wonderland. I want... I just want to go back for a while."

"Whatever you desire, Duchess." Kori said, his voice full of innuendo.

I rolled my eyes, but motioned toward my bags, "Let's go."

Alice hugged me, before whispering, "Be safe, Vivica Rose. And I hope you find what you're looking for out there."

I hugged her back tightly, before summoning a portal. "Time to go to Earth, boys."

I didn't look back to make sure they were following me as I stepped through the portal, breathing in the thinner Earth air with fresh lungs. I was going to explore this world and the next until I found all the broken parts of myself and managed to glue them back together. Edik, Kori, and Ledger wouldn't stop me from doing that.

Acknowledgements

I truly cannot believe the Reclaiming Wonderland series is finally complete. I've spent so many years with these characters; it has been bittersweet saying goodbye. I hope you feel that I gave Alice and her men the ending they deserved.

It's time to thank the amazing people who have supported me on this journey. From my husband and our families to Cantrell's Chaos Team, to Larissa my amazing artist. Each and every person helped me bring this book to you as the best version of itself. This book was an eighteen-month labor of love. I stressed every day making this book perfect. The support of my family, friends, and team truly made all the difference in the world I would never have finished it without them.

The people I want to thank most though is my readers. The wait for this book was long, and I can only hope you are satisfied. Words cannot express how much it means to me that you have supported my author journey so far.

About the author

Taila Cantrell can be found lurking in the mountains of East Tennessee with her husband. Whether she's at her day job, wrangling the feral blue-collar men, tucked into a local bookstore, or at home curled up with her many cats and two pups, she's always plotting the next story. Her readers can look forward to many genres from fantasy romance to poetry to murder mysteries there is no story Taila isn't willing to give her voice to.

In every story, Taila blends spellbinding romance with trauma, chaos, and hope. Her books remind readers that even in the darkest moments, the heart still remembers how to burn bright.

Also by

The Reclaiming Wonderland Series
Code Red
Code White: Frosted Wonderland
Blue Dreams
Emerald Knights

The Austral Witches:
Primal Echoes
One Bloody Night
Two Shadowed Hearts
Three Little Doves
Four Twisted Dreams
Five Burnt Offerings (Coming June 2026)

Mercy Valley:
Wing of the Dragon
Howl of the Wolf (Coming Soon)

Standalones
Ink and Chaos: A Poetry Collection
Slipper of Silver, Collar of Gold (Coming September 2026)